IMPORTANT PEOPLE

Astrid Gormsdottir (aged 14) ᛅᛋᚱᛁᚦᚱ:ᚴᚢᚱᛘᛋᚦᚢᛁᚱ	A Danish princess
Leif Ibrahimsson (aged 14) ᛚᛁᚠᚱ:ᛁᛒᚱᛅᚼᛁᛘᛋᚢᚾ	A would-be skald
Gorm the Old ᚴᚢᚱᛘᚱ:ᚴᛅᛘᛚ	Astrid's father, King of the Danes
Thyre Danebud ᚦᛋᚢᚱᚢᛁ:ᛏᛅᚾᛘᛅᚱᚴᛅᛦ:ᛒᚢᛏ	Gorm's queen, second wife, and mother of his children
Knut Gormsson (aged 23) ᚴᚾᚢᛏ:ᚴᚢᚱᛘᛋᚢᚾ	Their eldest son and heir; Gothi of Jelling
Haralt Gormsson (aged 20) ᚼᛅᚱᛅᛚᛏᚱ:ᚴᚢᚱᛘᛋᚢᚾ	The second of Gorm and Thyre's three children
Folkmar ᚠᚢᛚᚴᛘᛅᚱ	A Saxon missionary

SOME WORDS

Dane-mark	The borderlands and islands between Denmark and Sweden
Draugur	An angry, evil, awakened corpse
Gothi	A pagan priest
Hel	The land of (most of) the dead
Hnefatafl	A board game similar to chess
Ragnarok	The final, world-ending battle of gods and giants
Skald	A court poet
Thing	Law court and popular gathering
Thrall	Slave

THE YELLING STONES

OSKAR JENSEN

HOT
KEY
BOOKS

First published in Great Britain in 2015 by Hot Key Books
Northburgh House, 10 Northburgh Street, London EC1V 0AT

A CIP catalogue record for this book is available from the British Library.

ISBN: 978-1-4714-0411-5

1

This book is typeset in 11pt Sabon using Atomik ePublisher

Printed and bound by Clays Ltd, St Ives Plc

www.hotkeybooks.com

Hot Key Books is part of the Bonnier Publishing Group
www.bonnierpublishing.com

For Nils Jensen

'In the long-before – the bad old days when men wore hair all over, nothing more, and spirits stalked about, and all men saw – this land was given over to the bear, the wolf, the boar. There lived three sisters in those days, one large, one squat, one thin; and whether they were troll or witch, or both, no one knew, but it's certain that they kept their own company, and were seen only at night.

'That was for the best, for they wore their hair long to their toes. Thick and matted it was too, with flies and worse things in, and never cut, so all you could see were the ends of their lumpen noses, and sometimes, a dark eye.

'Well, one midwinter's night, they crept from the woods to a sacred place – it fairly reeked of power – and there they formed a circle, and began to make a spell. And such a spell it was: a hex to crack this land apart and lay it at their taloned, warty feet. And as they worked it, they sucked the strength from the earth below and the trees around, so *that they smiled wickedly behind their hair. Soon enough, all that power felt that good, that they just had to yell for the joy of it. A little more, and the world would be theirs.*

'But all that magic must have made them a touch slow, for they lost their heads for time, and right before the work was done, the weakling winter sun arose and turned them into stones. One large, one squat, one thin: the Yelling Stones, frozen fast, and the yell itself – a mad, terrible, powerful thing – hanging in the air between them. Hanging forever on the edge of glory.'

ONE

ᛁᚻ

Denmark, 958 AD

It was the first day of spring. The Yelling Stones, snow-swaddled, loomed before the great hall that bore their name and waited for something to happen. It would not take long. A short ride south-west, Astrid Gormsdottir was shouting to the sky.

'Stay your hand, dark power, for I am queen of the spring, and I forbid night to fall without my leave!'

'Oh, how can you say such things, Astrid? And as if you could have a midsummer night with snow still lying. Why, there's no more difference between the first day of spring and the last day of winter, than between . . . than between . . .'

'You know what, Bekkhild, I'm going to keep riding until you can think of a decent end to that sentence. I'll probably have to go on into tomorrow morning,' said Astrid.

And with that, Astrid spurred her horse away from her

1

companion, and the little group of servants following behind.

'Astrid,' shouted Bekkhild, 'do come back! It'll be dark soon. You're sure to get lost, and the king will be *furious*.' But Astrid never heard: the words were lost on the wind.

She was a young girl, tall, slender, and well wrapped up against the cold, with fur at her shoulders and a fur cap above, her thick gold plait streaming out behind as she urged her mount down the slope, towards the trees.

'Come on, Hestur,' said Astrid, to her snow-white horse. 'If you're just a little faster, we can leave them behind, and then we'll be alone – at last! We'll trot towards the gorge, follow the river round, and come up behind the hall, hidden in the forest the whole time.'

She pulled one glove off with her teeth to stroke Hestur's mane and neck. Coarse hair and hard muscles strong beneath her fingers. Bending low, she murmured in his ear. 'Then I'll give you a fine gallop over the plain to Jelling, and I bet we beat them back as well!'

The horse snorted, and bucked its way downhill, where the snow lay less thick beneath the spreading branches, the first green shoots peeping through the white. Astrid whooped, urging him on.

Bekkhild sighed, and pointed her mare down the hill. 'Urgh, that Astrid!' she said. 'Why is it always me that has to watch her . . . ?'

Astrid had never felt more free. Air stung her cheeks. Her thighs smarted from lack of practice. It was all so . . . so *alive*. 'As if I'm going to spend my first day outside plodding along with Bekkhild the boring, after *months* cooped up in the hall, when we could go *anywhere*! Just you and me, Hestur: you and me and the whole of the North to ride in!'

On and on, and soon the cries, and the soft thudding of snow-muffled hoofs, died away behind them. Girl and horse rode alone between tall oaks, ash and beeches. Astrid loved the trees. Their tall trunks, rank upon rank, could be a guard of honour. She sat a little straighter in the saddle, small chin and snub nose tilted up to acknowledge her loyal tree-followers.

But once the first thrill of solitude was passed, she came back to herself, and frowned. 'I wish you'd go a bit faster, Hestur,' she said. 'It's not half so light as it was, and we should have hit the river long ago . . .'

She broke off as a rushing sound grew louder, and soon the sight she expected lay before them: the ground falling away to their right, tumbling down a high gorge to churning water, made thick by melting snows. White willows bent their heads, and trailed slender fingers in the stream.

Astrid smiled and nudged Hestur left along the valley, but it was a thin smile: the shadows were longer now, pooling to a general darkness.

That was when she heard the first howl.

Instantly Hestur's ears were up and his nostrils flared. Astrid too was bolt upright and tense, but she forced herself to lay a hand on the horse's neck and whisper. 'There now, boy, one wolf's no worry for the likes of us. But it's time to be getting home. Come on . . . Come *on*, Hestur!' For his legs were rooted in the snow and he would not heed her, even when she dug in her heels. And now his ears lay flat, ready for the danger.

3

Cross with the horse and with herself for losing track of time, Astrid tried to think of what to do next. But all she could think of were hard yellow eyes, sharp teeth, and all the times when she'd been little, and cried at the dark.

Another howl, deeper than the first, came from somewhere in front of them. It was answered away to their left, and then again, behind, louder still. Or, was that two howls together?

Astrid was fumbling at her waist for her long knife when it happened. A snarling at their left and Hestur bolted, twisting to the right, lurching down the sheer falls of rock towards the river. He was spooked, hoofs skittering on the soft edge of the gorge. Loose stones tumbled into darkness and Astrid clung to his neck, every bit as terrified, certain they would fall.

If she squeezed shut her eyes and only held on, everything might still be all right.

And then – thank the gods – they were down, and going slowly, and she could raise her head and open her eyes.

A wolf was looking back at her.

Astrid choked back a scream. *You're enormous*, she thought, but she couldn't be sure. He was black enough to be little more than a burning pair of eyes in the night – it was *definitely* night-time now – and near enough that he might spring.

Just then she felt a lapping at her feet and almost jumped out of the saddle, before realising that Hestur had backed into the river itself. The dark water ran around her ankles, deathly cold.

The big wolf sank back on its haunches and opened its

jaws. The howling was all around them, on both banks, a whole pack, emboldened by the long lean winter and their gnawing white hunger. The brute in front of her arched its back, winding up like a horrid hairy coil.

Astrid drew her knife. *I'm just a girl*, she thought. The wolf sprang.

Then it was bright hot and the red flame all around. Smoke stung her eyes and made her head swim, so she thought she saw a boy, brandishing fire in each hand, the wolves shrinking from the burning torches.

'Away, troll-steeds! You, Gauti's hound, and you, sun-swallower! Slink off the lot of you, harm-crew of the forest; lope off and slake your blood-thirst at some other feast!'

'What the *Hel*?!' said Astrid. For there *was* a boy, and now he turned, his head wreathed by the flames. The wolves were gone. Hestur surged onto the bank, towards their rescuer. The boy smiled – a nice smile, she thought.

And then he fell to the ground, and started screaming.

:

Then there were voices, people, dogs and horses: Bekkhild; Odd and Bredi – the thralls who had ridden out behind them – and someone had taken up Hestur's reins from where they hung, neglected.

'Wolves?' someone was asking, and, 'Are you hurt?'

And there was Bekkhild, saying, 'And what's wrong with *him*?'

Astrid shook her head clear. She saw the boy spreadeagled on his back, thrashing his limbs, half in and half out of the water. Whether that was foam on his lips, or spray from the river, was hard to tell in so little light.

'And who *is* he?'

'He's in a trance!'

'You'd think a trance would be quieter . . .'

His whole body shook as if worried by a dog, and he was roaring loud enough to shame the wolves. Astrid blinked, shrugged her shoulders, pulled herself together. Time to act like her father's daughter.

'That's the boy who rescued me,' she said. 'Lay him across your horse, Bredi; you can share with Odd. We shall take him back to Jelling.'

TWO

ᛏᚢᛁᚱ

The news arrived before them, for Astrid, still shaken, kept pace with the witless boy, and Bekkhild and the others rushed ahead, eager for warmth, shelter and attention. The grubby faces of the grooms were lit with curiosity as they handed Astrid lightly down, and hauled the boy off Bredi's horse with rather less grace. 'Bring him,' she said to the thralls, and strode into the hall of Gorm the Old.

'Was it wolves then, Astrid?'

'You silly girl!'

'Have you captured an elf on your ride, child?'

The evening's feasting had begun, and a hundred insolent revellers crowded in on her, closing out the fresh spring air with their faces, their questions, and their bad breath. Chin up, Astrid ignored the voices that came at her from either side, as she walked between the central fires and the long earth banks against the walls that served as benches. She hoped that anyone who saw her red cheeks in the dim light, flushed with embarrassment, would put it down to the coldness of the night and the heat of the hall. But oh, how she *hated* returning to that crammed, heaving hall; the dark, stinking, smoky prison of her every winter.

They wouldn't dare address me like that if I were a boy, she thought, and then, *I am so very, very hungry*. Out loud, she muttered a tetchy 'Hurry up,' to Odd and Bredi, who were carrying the boy.

The hall was long: there was none so large in all the North lands. Sweat dripped from red faces, and in dark corners, dogs worried discarded gristle. Somewhere above, between dark rafters, scuttled little spirits that you never saw – tiny guardians of the hall, who slunk down at night to finish the food and sip the dregs from the drinking-horns. People, dogs, spirits: the place was so *crowded* . . .

Astrid's lungs were itching from the fumes and her slim legs were trembling, but at last she was nearing the end. Before her loomed the dais, a platform the width of the hall, floored with oak planks rather than beaten earth, and there, beyond the high table – hard to see for all the smoke, fragrant with the scent of juniper and spruce, and for the shadows that crept from dark corners – there on a craggy throne of greying ash – his silvered beard sweeping the tabletop – there was her father.

Astrid looked up, and though all eyes were on her she was aware only of his: grey, watery, failing, yet still the eyes of a king.

But it was not King Gorm who spoke first. A voice cut in from Astrid's right – 'I hear someone got lost playing in the woods.'

She glared, stung out of her silence. 'I was not lost,' she said. 'The wolves had come right up, this side of the gorge. They've never done that before.'

'And of course you're old enough to say "never",' replied the voice. It was dry, amused, dusty: the speaker was her brother, Haralt. Tall and gaunt, he had their father's long nose, but as yet, only a straggly blond excuse for a beard. At twenty, he was just six years her elder, and Astrid was on the point of a still angrier reply, when a rumbling cough, like distant thunder, came from the depths of the silver beard before her. King Gorm was ready to speak.

'Dumb brutes would never come so close. When wolves lose their fear like this, there's sure to be a witch-rider at the back of it, spurring them on. That's the problem with living by the Yelling Stones – you get all sorts of creatures, drawn to their power.'

'Really, Father,' replied Haralt, 'I wish you'd drop this notion that witches ride wolves like we ride horses. *I've* certainly never seen such a thing.'

'Small wonder,' another voice broke in, now from Astrid's left. This one was low, almost a growl: Knut, her eldest brother, sat at the king's right hand. He looked like he sounded: big, brown and shaggy. Gold glinted on his massive upper arms.

'How would *you* ever see a witch-rider, brother,' Knut went on, 'when you've never seen fit to come on a wolf hunt! Speaking of which, I may as well take a gang out tomorrow. The men could use a good hunt after sleeping through the winter. Why don't you come along, Haralt, and see if you can bag the witch yourself?'

'Some of us have more important things to do than running round the woods, chasing stories,' said Haralt. 'And I'll add this, Knut: if you *do* think you spot a witch, then ask yourself how many horns of ale you've drunk that day before telling any tall tales.'

Astrid sighed. This was shaping up into a typical row – the brothers had never got on. Usually at this point, she shut up and pretended not to exist. It always worked; everyone else somehow seemed to be pretending the same thing. But not this time. She owed it to her rescuer to seize the king's attention.

'Father,' she said, raising her voice above Knut's next words, 'I have brought the boy who saved me. He deserves much honour . . . but . . . but something has happened to him . . .'

'Bring him forward. Let's see this saviour of yours.' Again, it was not the king who spoke, but the last of the four who were sat on the dais, this time immediately at the king's left. Queen Thyre.

'Here he is, Mother,' said Astrid, and motioned the thralls forward with their burden. The hall was silent now, so quiet that Astrid imagined she could hear the craning of necks as men fought for a better view.

She had the best view of all, and jumped at the sight. The boy's eyes had opened, but just the whites – his pupils had rolled round inside his head – and his tongue lolled from his gaping mouth.

Haralt tittered at Astrid's obvious discomfort.

'He's in a trance,' said her mother, ignoring her second

10

son. She raised her voice. It was high, lofty, commanding. 'What do you see, boy?'

'I see you, Thyre, adornment of the Dane-mark.'

Astrid was not the only one to start at this; the boy spoke like two rocks rending, and it was awful to see, for his lips never moved.

'And I see you, King Gorm, Knut, Haralt, Astrid – all those in this hall, and all their womenfolk and children. But I do not see the hall itself: we walk, a thousand strong, down a road between high mountains.'

'A vision,' someone muttered.

'Hush,' came a reply.

The boy never paused. 'Now there is a boiling river ahead. It spits and froths, coming ever closer. Here the road forks; I know not which to choose.'

So terrible was his manner of speech, that all hung on his words.

'The left leads to a man, who stands alone. His skin is dark; his robes are thin and white; he wears a crown of thorns upon his head. He says we have to walk on the water. The right hand path ends with a ferryman; his raft is broad enough to take us all. This man is old, and leans upon his staff – his face is hid beneath a broad-brimmed hat.

'So now I move towards him – but some danger blots the sun! A thing with wings descends upon the man, who raises up his staff to fend it off. The creature beats about him, tries to strike . . . I cannot see . . . the sun is going . . . I cannot reach him . . .'

The boy was frothing once again, windmilling his arms and

11

trying to rise. Astrid was shouldered roughly aside as Odd and Bredi rushed to restrain him, each taking hold of an arm.

Thyre stood up. 'Awake!' she said, in the imperious tone she had used before.

At once, the boy snapped upright, quivering like a knife thrown point-first to the ground. Then he stumbled, slumped between his carriers, all tension fled from his body. His eyes opened again, and this time Astrid saw that they were normal. Large, dark, intelligent – but normal for all that. When he spoke, his voice was rough with the effort, yet pleasant enough otherwise.

'Where am I?' was all he said.

'Jelling,' replied Thyre. She paused. 'Or possibly, at a path by a river – you've been relating a vision. Do you remember?'

'Perhaps . . .'

'The second man was, of course, the great god Odin,' Thyre mused. 'In all the stories, he travels in the disguise of a blind ferryman. And you, my liege,' she said, turning to Gorm, 'are famed as Odin's man.'

'That's true enough,' said Gorm. 'The King of the Danes should worship the king of the gods.'

'But what attacked him? An eagle?' said Knut. 'Who could that be?'

'Haakon of Norway?' said Haralt. 'He's already caused my friends a deal of harm. Or, of course, it could be just a boy dreaming about a bird.'

'What about the other man?' said Astrid. 'The one with the funny crown?' But her voice was small, and no one at the high table heard her.

12

'The eagle could mean King Otto,' said Knut, almost to himself. 'The Saxon always seeks to rule the Dane.'

'We don't even know it's an eagle,' said Thyre.

'Enough!' rumbled Gorm. 'Two paths for my kingdom, and Odin under attack: clearly, there is much to think on here. For now, my mind would move to other things. You have spoken for the gods, lad. Have you anything to say for yourself?'

Astrid looked back at the boy. The discussion at the high table had given him a chance to catch his breath. He was visibly more confident as he spoke.

'Honour to you, great Gorm,
And good health to your hall.
I'm brought before heroes,
Borne on Odin's longship.'

'He's a poet!' cried Knut.

'"Odin's longship" – he means a horse,' Gorm mumbled in delight, to no one in particular.

The boy smiled.

'Wise ears await my tale,
Words to bring the spring forth.
Come to pledge and praise you,
Parched am I for malt-surf.'

'Bring the boy ale,' roared Gorm. 'I find he has a tongue swift enough to merit much whetting!'

'Very well put, o King of the Jotar,' said the boy. A drinking horn was placed in his hand, full of a foaming liquid.

Astrid, standing ignored at his shoulder, eyed it enviously.

Not only was he hogging her father's attention, but now he was being served before her – and she was a princess!

'Share my beer horn? I'd deem it a favour.' The boy turned to Astrid, offering the horn, eyes downcast.

Astrid giggled nervously, and took a deep draught. *Well,* she thought, *he* did *save me, after all.*

As if reading her thoughts, Haralt spoke. 'It seems we owe you thanks, little skald, for getting this girl out of quite a mess.'

'Why don't you both join us at the table, and eat and drink your fill?' said Queen Thyre, and turned to her husband. 'Whatever size the debt this boy is due, it can begin with a meal, free from questions, can't it?'

Gorm, still chuckling to himself, nodded his assent, gesturing them forward with a sweep of one bony, jewelled hand. Now there were six at the high table: Astrid's parents, her two brothers, herself . . . and the stranger.

'Thanks for this, sweet Thyre; thoughtful is your judgement,' said the boy, all in a rush. Only it sounded more like 'thoughtful is your thudge-um' because his mouth was full of food before he finished speaking.

THREE

ᚦᚱᛁᛦ

'You're not used to such fare, I'll wager,' growled Knut, the older prince. The boy had eaten all that was placed before him – sausage, salt beef, bacon, and bowl upon bowl of vegetable soup – and drunk his horn of ale, and now he was clearly in trouble, hands clasped over a tight-stretched stomach.

Astrid, pleasantly full herself, looked at him fondly. He was going to be sick, she decided, if not now then later, and his face should surely be white – only his skin was so strangely dark . . .

'No, Knut Gormsson, I'm not used to it,' the boy said.

'Well at least it's got you talking normally, and not in verse,' said Haralt. 'And it appears you hold an advantage over us. For you have our names, whilst for all we know, you're a thrall or an outlaw!'

Haralt laughed, showing his teeth, two of which were chiselled across and filled with a deep blue dye after the

15

current fashion. They'd started calling him 'Haralt Bluetooth' already – a nickname Astrid thought he preferred far more than being known as simply the son of Gorm. Now she shuddered. She knew that laugh well, and there was not a trace of kindness in it.

'My name is Leif, lord,' said the boy.

'Leif what?'

'Just Leif. And –' here the boy smiled through his discomfort – 'the story of my missing name is well worth hearing. If I could maybe step outside for a moment first?'

'The bogs are that way, lad,' said Knut, pointing down the hall. More laughter spread at the speed of his flight.

Told you so, thought Astrid.

Soon Leif returned, walking at a more respectable pace. Astrid had a proper look at him. He was as slim as her, but his face was all hard lines where hers was soft curves, and he had a shock of thick dark hair that rose, unruly, from his head. He was dressed in a plain but well-cut tunic belted with twine, and rough woollen hose: he could easily pass for the son of a farmer or craftsman. *Not* a thrall, she decided. But not a noble either. Where had he learnt to speak so well?

'Let's have your story then,' said Knut.

Gorm sighed in anticipation. Haralt sank back, and took out his ivory toothpick. Astrid sat close to her mother and leant in, half hoping for an arm around her shoulder. Thyre smiled distractedly, patting Astrid's shoulder for a moment, then turned back towards Leif. The boy took a deep breath, and began.

'You ask me, Haralt Gormsson, why I lack a father's

name. More than that, I lack a father. Whoever my parents were, when I was born I must have struck them as strange, for they left me in the forest, that the wolves might have something sweeter than deer for their supper that night. But it was no wolf that found me, so I'm told, but the red-furred sheep-destroyer. A she-fox poked and chivvied me, and rolled me to her earth. It may have been she had no kits, and took me for her own.

'There I dwelt, beneath the ground, and suckled for a time. And there was fox's mischief in her milk, for one day, so they say, I must have set off by myself. A tiny, naked, hairless thing, rooting round in the dark. I crawled, not up, but down that hole, pushing soil aside. I wandered long past roots and rocks, surprising worms and busy moles, driven ever deeper, seeking after warmth . . .

'Well, when I was deeper than a baby's ever been, I found my progress halted by a crumbling wall of loam. Either I didn't much care for going back up, or the soft, cloying feel of that soil between my fingers gave me pleasure, but I soon broke it apart, and, blinking, pushed on through . . .

'Only to tumble down, down, down! Down I fell through a cavern higher than this hall, and such a sight it must have been, a muddy babe flung from the skies, plummeting ever faster, till – plop! – I landed in a churn of milk!'

Knut snorted.

Astrid leant forward. 'A churn of milk? Under the ground?'

'Hush, child,' said Gorm, and motioned for Leif to continue.

'Stubby hands fished me out, dripping wet and white.

17

And it's this that forms my earliest memory: black and bearded faces, knobbled noses, pebbled eyes and toothy grins. Dwarfs!'

'Dwarfs, indeed!' said Haralt. 'It's a wonder this addled speech-maker didn't claim to fall into the mead of Kvasir – the magic drink that gave poetry to the gods.' But Haralt too was shushed by Gorm.

'It's they who raised me,' said Leif. 'And taught me rhymes, and stories too, and showed me how to work metals with my hands – but not too well, for fear that I'd teach others, and their secrets would be out. Uri and Skirvir taught me this craft, and Thulinn and Fjalarr taught me to speak. Solblindi helped me to walk in the dark, and Hilding showed me the ways of the sword. Naef gave me my name, Leif, which – as you know – means "descendant". For, so he said, he'd never seen such a descent as when I fell from the roof! If I wanted any other name, he said, I'd have to win it for myself.'

'That's wise,' said Knut.

'Fourteen summers passed, and I saw not one,' said Leif, 'but lived always in that cavern. That's where I got this swarthy skin of mine, from being raised by black dwarfs underground.'

'And then what? You dug your way back up again?' said Haralt with a yawn.

'Ingi and Lofarr, and Alfrigg, who rules there, deemed it the time for my living with men. They had a task for me to do besides; it's they who wish to honour you, King Gorm. First, I was sworn to never show the way, and then they led me by a secret path, and set me on the road to your domain.'

'The dwarfs acknowledge me?' said Gorm.

'Yes – and your right to rule in all the North.'

'All the North!' cried Gorm. 'Hear him! And why should I not still crush the Swedes, and Haakon of Norway, beneath my mighty heel?! I'm not so old as all that, after all.'

'In other words,' said Haralt, 'you've come up here, a nameless child with a tall story, to chance your arm at court. You might as well have promised us the sky's allegiance, or that of the birds.'

'You know, Haralt,' chuckled Knut, 'those would be fine gifts indeed, if one could prove it!'

'But, lords, I can. I bring a gift,' said Leif.

Astrid gasped. She just couldn't help herself. From nowhere, so it seemed, the boy had brought forth a sword. How, just *how*, had he done that?

Men were on their feet now, down the length of the hall, clapping at the trick, or crying witchcraft. Knut snatched up the blade.

'Weland,' he called to a man on the benches, 'come take a look at this! I'll swear you've never seen its like. Nor could you craft its twin, for all your skill!'

The man Weland, Jelling's smith, came up to the table. As he leant across Astrid to take the sword from Knut, she caught the reek of sulphur on his clothes and wrinkled up her nose.

Weland whistled. 'If any other man had spoke those words, Knut Gormsson, and about any other weapon, he'd find its point between his ribs for the offence. But this! I've never seen its equal. It must have been just such a blade as this that Reginn forged for Sigurd long ago.'

19

He laid it down along the table, and at last Astrid could see properly.

Well, what did she expect – it was a sword. But she knew something about swords, and couldn't help echoing Weland's whistle. An uncommonly bright, blueish blade, with a wicked looking edge, and the finest hilt she'd ever seen. Inscribed along the blade and picked out, all in gold, were strange and subtle characters, flowing and flicking.

'These are not runes,' she said, 'nor Christian letters.'

'Dwarf words,' breathed Knut, his eyes shining. 'They must hold great power.'

Gorm brought his skeletal fist crashing down on the table, and they all leapt back from the bouncing blade, snatching away their fingers.

Astrid risked a quick glance into her father's face. If the impact had pained him, as she felt sure it had, his rheumy old eyes gave nothing away.

'Let it be known I accept this gift,' said King Gorm. 'Boy, I name you Skald-Leif for your skill with words. You are to have a seat on my benches here, between Weland the smith and Arinbjorn the Unlucky, and the sword shall hang in the royal bedchamber.'

Gorm clutched at the weapon, and shuffled from the hall. Thyre gave a tight-lipped smile to her children, and to Leif, before hurrying after her husband.

Knut turned to the boy, patting him on the back. 'Tell you what, little "Skald-Leif". Since you're so good with wolves, why don't you come along on my hunt tomorrow, eh? Then maybe you can make up a poem about my skill!

Who knows, you might even kill one yourself . . .'

Knut broke off, puzzled, to find Leif sprawled on the floor. The back-pat from the prince's huge paw of a hand had knocked him flying.

'. . . Or, maybe you can just tag along and watch,' Knut finished.

Haralt's laugh echoed from the beams above; even Astrid hid a grin. The feast was over.

FOUR

ᚠᛁᚪᚱᛁᚱ

By rights, thought Astrid, she should have slept for days after her encounter with the wolves – an adventure wholly overshadowed by Leif's story, and the sword. She felt dog-tired in all her slender limbs. But she had not slept. Wolves, dwarfs and brown-faced boys with bare-faced tales ran round and round her head.

How much of what he'd said was true? But then, hadn't he rescued her, back there at the river? Hadn't that earned him her trust? And exactly what had happened, when the black wolf sprung?

A quiet scurrying broke in on her thoughts. That would be Nisse, the hall-spirit who lived above her own room. She shared it during the winter with three older girls: Guma, Bekkhild, and Hyndla. The four of them slept in one of two side-chambers off the head-end of the hall. Knut and Haralt had the other, and her parents' room was behind the throne itself. As far as she knew, Nisse was the only male spirit;

22

those above the main hall were all female. Astrid always left milk out for the strange, unseen little creature. In return, he chased away rats, patched up holes in the roof, and – she was fairly sure of this – spied on the girls when they were getting undressed. The feast must have made him restless, and now his noise was threatening to wake the others.

'Astrid?' moaned Guma, still three-quarters asleep.

The three girls were technically her handmaidens, daughters of some of Gorm's jarls, over-wintering at Jelling. The jarls were the foremost men in the kingdom, so the girls were more like sisters than servants.

But more like witches than either, thought Astrid. None of the others left Nisse anything, and in revenge he sometimes dropped acorns on their heads to keep them awake. Astrid encouraged this. The girls were the bane of her life, and could do with a sleepless night now and then.

But right now, that was the last thing Astrid wanted, and she glared up into the rafters. She herself had given up all thoughts of dropping off – she had to put her head straight. But to lie awake, in that musty room, hemmed in by snores? Never! She had to get outside, where there was room to breathe. And if Guma woke up, she'd be sure to stop her.

Softly, Astrid rose to her feet, tiptoed to the far wall and tugged on her supple goatskin boots. Her overdress – blue-dyed wool lined with black sable – was slung across a chest, and now she pulled it on over her linen shift, wincing at the clinking of the brooches.

The only door led to the main hall: a man was posted there to guard the girls at night. But behind the chest, hidden by a heavy tapestry of tangled serpent-beasts, was a loose plank in the oaken outer wall. Astrid had long since worked at it with her knife, till she was sure of swinging it aside when escape was called for. One quick squeak of wood and nail, a rush of icy air, and she was free. Now, she could think about –

'Astrid?'

This time, she was sure, it was Leif who called – she'd heard enough of his voice that evening to know it by now. He was somewhere ahead of her, to the east, in the darkness. He must be by the stones.

Of course, he would be. No one new to Jelling could resist their pull.

'Can you feel them, Astrid?' he called.

She padded forward through the pale snow, gulping at the crisp night air. By the snow's light, reflecting that of the wan moon above, she caught sight of his slight, shadowy form, closer than she'd thought. Maybe now she'd have some answers.

'Hello, Leif,' she said.

He seemed to accept their presence out there, in the dead of night, without question.

She didn't. 'What are you doing up?'

Instead of answering her, he pointed at the three silent shapes, looming before them. 'Tell me about the stones,' he said.

'Not until I'm satisfied,' she said. 'Was all that true, what you said earlier? Were you really raised by dwarfs?'

'Your father took me at my word,' he said, still not turning to look at her. 'I'd hope that would be good enough for you.'

'And your vision – the river, the two paths, all that?'

'In truth I cannot really remember. It was more than a dream. But more than *that* . . . I cannot say. I have never had such a trance before.'

'Next question then. The sword you brought my father, from the dwarfs: is that the only reason you came to Jelling?'

'Are you questioning my motives, Astrid?'

'Not really. I'm just curious. Still, if you don't want to talk openly, I'm sure you can find someone else to tell you about the stones . . .' She made as if to leave.

'No, Astrid, wait!' He caught her arm. But it was his dark eyes that held her at his side.

'I had my own reasons, I admit it,' he said. 'It's a chance to make my name in the world. Gorm is the richest and most powerful king in all the North, and the skald who sings his praises might do very well for himself, as well as for his king. But I'm not just out for an easy life. They say Egil Skallagrimsson, the greatest skald in all the North, has sailed for Iceland for the last time. That means there's a chance for younger poets to win fame for themselves, and where better to try than at Jelling?'

She nodded. 'That's why I'd be here, if I were you,' she said. 'And besides, you had that vision, whatever it was about. Maybe the gods sent you as a warning of some sort.'

'I don't know about that,' he said. 'I don't much care for being sent to do another's will. I'd far rather forget that trance, and simply be myself.'

'I know exactly what you mean,' she said. 'All right, one last question, then I'll tell you what you want to know. So:

of course you know my brothers' names. The swaggering sons of the King of the Danes, everyone's heard of them. But no one outside Jelling knows who *I* am. How did you find out my name?'

'I guessed,' he said. 'Astrid means "god's beauty". It seemed likely.' Well. She hadn't been expecting *that*.

'They're . . . they're the Yelling Stones,' she said, to cover her embarrassment. 'They've been here forever, or near enough, since before the first kings anyway, and they're meant to be three troll-women, caught by the sun in the middle of a spell. That big-boned one at the east of their circle was a queen, I think, and the short one nearer us, and the tall one to the right, her sisters. They were shouting words of power – *immense* power – when they froze, and Jelling's been a source of power ever since.'

Without even looking, Astrid felt Leif's eyes upon her. He was paying *very* close attention . . . She flushed, and hurried on. 'That's why father built his hall here: people have always been attracted to their magic. See that mound, off to the left? The land's earliest rulers lie buried there. Hundreds of years ago, chieftains made Jelling their home. Now we've come here, and Father's made himself king: it's no coincidence. All this wealth – the hall, stables, baths and farms – you think it came from nowhere? My grandfather used to sleep with his pigs to keep warm before we came to Jelling.'

Astrid was gesturing around them as she spoke. 'And then there's this broken arc of rocks – see there, and there, under the snow?'

She pointed to a toothy string of stones, smaller than the three before them, but ancient nonetheless. 'The giants built a stone ship here, in the old days, to sail over Bifrost Bridge and see the gods. Or something like that – I had all this off old Bragi Bragisson. He was the last skald here, before you, but he died some years back; that's why you've got the job . . .'

She broke off, and blushed, suddenly aware of how long she had spoken, and how poor it must have sounded to the poet at her side.

She snuck a look. Leif was glowing with excitement.

'Strange things happen at Jelling,' she went on, encouraged. 'We get more than our fair share of elves and witches round here: they can't resist the lure of the stones. And Bragi – the poet who died – had this one story of an old king, buried in the mound. At every full moon, he said, the light catches the stones *just so*, and the whole place becomes so awash in magic that the old king's corpse – his draugur – gets up and hammers on the mound to be let out! I half believed him at the time.'

She half believed it even now. A long-dead king, black and massive, stirring from his rest inside the earth – it was deliciously horrible.

'I've never seen a dwarf, though,' she said. 'What are they like?'

'I can feel the stones, Astrid!' He must have not heard her question. 'Is the magic still strong, then?' he asked.

'Hah!' She couldn't help but shudder. 'Just ask old Bragi Bragisson!'

'I thought you just said he was dead?' said Leif, frowning.

'But can you guess *how* he died?' Astrid was starting to enjoy herself. 'Of course, I was just a little girl, but I'll never forget it.'

'So tell me.'

'It's always been said that the strength of the stones is there for the taking. That one day, someone strong enough to stand between the stones and brave the yell will come to Jelling and make himself their master. The one who harnessed that power would have the whole of the North at his feet.'

'To stand between the stones? But that's easy,' said Leif, and stepped forward.

The weird grey shapes were monstrous in the moonlight, and their dark embrace was a step away from Leif when Astrid leapt on him.

'Stop!' she cried, hauling him back from the silent circle.

'What's wrong?' He looked angry, she thought, angry enough that he might hit her, and there was hunger in his expression.

'That's just what Bragi tried to do,' she explained. 'He spent his whole life here, learning all there was to know about the Yelling Stones, making up poems . . . some say he even spoke to them. And they spoke back, I mean. At last, he thought he was ready. He thought he could withstand the stones. All he did was stop up his ears with beeswax. I'll never forget that day.'

Astrid's eyes were bright at the memory. She lowered her voice. 'It was at midsummer, seven years ago. In front of all the court, Bragi walked between the stones.'

'So what *happened*, Astrid?'

She smiled in spite of herself. Never had anyone hung on her words like this before – let alone a proven poet. But then the memory rose before her again, and the smile sagged. She had been standing just where she was now . . . Back then, of course, she'd been only seven . . .

'Bragi strode into the middle of the circle. The sun was shining; he was dressed in red; the whole court was happy, because the old skald had pledged any power he might win to Father, before he started. For an instant he stood there at his ease; it seemed like nothing could go wrong.'

She sighed. 'But he couldn't do it. For all his years of work, Bragi couldn't master the stones. First, he frowned. And then he clapped his hands to his ears . . .'

It was odd. She was almost enjoying this. But it had been one of the worst moments of her life. For weeks afterwards she'd had hot, sweaty nightmares and run to her mother. And now here she was, spinning the tale to the strange boy.

'. . . And then he clapped his hands to his ears. I could see his face crumple and crack like dry wood in a fire. He sank to his knees, writhing, eyes popping from his head. He looked as lost, as ugly, as a bawling baby left on a hillside.'

'Didn't anybody try to help him?'

'What, and hear whatever he was hearing? Not likely! Anyway, in a few moments it was all over. First his skin went red as his cloak. Then it blistered. And then he was on fire, no longer a man but a flaming torch of flesh. I was forced back inside with the other children. But later, I saw what they dragged out from the circle – and I mean dragged;

they used boar-spears to reach in and hook it out – and it was a charred and blackened lump, twisted as a tree root, no bigger than a year-old lamb. That's the power of the Yelling Stones: the power, and the danger.'

Astrid blinked as she finished, surprised to see how much lighter the night had become. It was nearly dawn.

For a moment, neither spoke, but Leif's eyes never left her own. His jaw had dropped open.

So, she thought. *That's what it's like to be really listened to. To be a skald.*

At last, Leif pulled himself together. 'One day,' he said, thrusting out his narrow chest, 'I'll step between those stones.'

She smiled, and turned to go.

'I will,' he said. 'I mean it!'

'Oh, I believe you,' she said, walking back to the hall.

'I will though.'

'Sure.'

'No, really! Really, I will . . .'

FIVE

ᚠᛁᛏ

'Astrid! Time to be up!' It was Bekkhild, of course. Who else could sound so annoying, so early in the morning? 'We've got *so* much sewing to do!'

A few moments later, Astrid slunk out of the hall. She hoped that, amid the general morning bustle, no one would notice Bekkhild's whines until she was well away. Her foot still throbbed from where she'd kicked the girl's shins, but it was a small price to pay for such an immense feeling of satisfaction.

She emerged into brilliant sunlight: the second day of spring was more awash in promise than the first.

Fat chance of me sitting around sewing, she thought. *If Leif's going to watch the wolf hunt, then so am I, and I'd like to see anyone try and stop me.*

She paused, thinking of how she was in fact always stopped on these occasions. If Leif saw her hoisted over Knut's shoulder like a sack of straw, and tossed back in the

31

hall, she'd never live it down. No; this called for subtler tactics.

'Ah, Astrid, there you are.' It was Haralt. She groaned. 'Aren't you supposed to be working on the new tapestry for the great hall?' he said. 'You know – to replace the one Knut threw up over at midwinter and they couldn't get the stains out.'

'Er . . .' She was caught, fair and square.

'Me? Throw up? I don't remember that.' It was Knut, strolling from the stables, leading a harnessed stallion.

Haralt turned to him. 'I'm not surprised, since you passed out a moment later!'

'Me? Pass out? I don't remember that.'

This was Astrid's chance. As her brothers began to argue, she slipped into the now deserted stable block. Good: no one had noticed. Hestur was alert, champing, aware that something was up. Tearing strips from a discarded rag, she bound them tight around his hoofs to muffle their sound. There. He was snow-white, her cloak was dark as a tree trunk – with luck, they'd blend in with the forest.

A mewling came from the darkness of the stall. It was Valvigs, her gyrfalcon, tethered to his perch. Astrid's heart went out to the beautiful white bird – her best friend, after Hestur – and she slipped the leather jesses from the perch to her wrist. He'd never forgive her if she left him behind: Valvigs hated being shut up for the winter every bit as much as she did.

'Just keep quiet, all right? If you go blowing our cover, then no mice for you for a month!'

Then she waited for her brothers to end their quarrel, the words carrying clear to where she hid.

'Well,' said Haralt, 'and where are your beaters? Your nets?'

Knut spat loudly. 'Real men don't need nets. Besides, I'm not sure Thorbjorn and the rest would know what to do with them; I'd spend half my time untangling my own men. No: spears and sharp senses are all we need, isn't that right, lads?'

A chorus of gruff cheers told Astrid the hunt was assembled.

'But surely,' Haralt persisted, 'some kind of *system* . . .'

'You speak more like a Christ-man than a true Dane, brother! But you'll learn in time. Which is just what I've not got: any more time. Thorbjorn, is everyone ready?'

'Aye, sire!' She knew the speaker: he was Knut's right-hand man. Big. Brave. A little dim.

'And, Leif, have you got that horse facing the right way yet?'

'I'm working on it, lord,' came the reply.

'Then we ride!'

The troop thundered out of the yard, sweeping south towards the forests where she'd met the wolves the day before. Astrid peered round the stable door, waiting for Haralt to storm off – it would never do to be caught a second time, especially with her brother smarting from Knut's careless words.

When all was clear, she swung herself lightly into Hestur's saddle, settled Valvigs on her wrist, and sped after the vanishing hunt.

Astrid dismounted as quietly as she could, looping Hestur's bridle round a young birch and then flattening herself against its trunk. A few trees away were the group: a dozen burly warriors . . . and Leif.

'We'll leave the horses here, and hunt on foot,' Knut was saying. 'Oh, Leif, I see you're a step ahead of me!'

She sniggered: not for the first time, the boy had fallen from his horse. Not that he was the only one having trouble keeping his seat; all the beasts were snorting, tossing their heads, half trying to buck their riders from the saddle. What was it they could smell on the chill spring wind?

Knut led off his hunting party, leaving a man behind to guard the horses. Astrid felt a pang at abandoning Hestur. 'But let's face it, you weren't *that* much use yesterday, were you?' she whispered. 'I'll make you a hot mash later, for your patience.' And she crept off after them, the falcon on her arm, padding lightly between the thickening trees.

She felt at home here. The northern sky, cut into shards by still-bare trunks, was hard and bright as sapphire, the rolling ground a soft blanket of white. You could imagine the forest going on forever, with never a wall to close you in.

But it didn't last. The more she crept uphill towards the gorge, the darker it became. A dank grey mist was rising from the ground.

Soon she had trouble keeping the others in sight. Soon,

it was like walking through cold porridge. This was never a natural mist.

Astrid was quite alone. The crack of a branch underfoot went right through her. Which way was she to go?

If she let her eyes drift, she could see shapes. Figures. Grey forms lurking in the corners of her eyes that would dart away when she turned. Not quite people, not quite animals. Beings made of mist, of magic, of her imagination.

That didn't make them any less frightening.

Silence; total silence. Even the sound of her own breathing was swallowed in greyness.

A dozen wolves could be watching her through the fog, and the first she'd know of it would be fangs ripping out her throat.

And then Valvigs erupted off her wrist: a shocking noise and flurry of wings, tumbling her to the ground. By the time she'd picked herself up, heart hammering, the falcon was nowhere to be seen.

Astrid took a few steps in what she thought was the way she'd come. Then she stopped.

Surely, those were *other* footsteps, other twigs cracking, a little way off. Or maybe 'footsteps' was the wrong word . . .

She drew her knife, more for comfort than from a belief it would really help, and hurried on. There *was* something keeping pace with her, a steady *pad pad pad*, somewhere out there, in the mist.

No, not keeping pace – coming closer.

She ran, not caring where she went, tripping over roots and blundering into branches. The unseen thing was gaining – it was ahead of her – and with an impact that drove the breath from her body, she ran right into –

'*Leif?!*' She was furious. 'I could have stabbed you! Why didn't you call out?'

'Astrid?' The boy was doubled over, winded. 'Astrid? Oh gods! I thought you were a wolf!'

'So did I . . . I mean, I thought *you* were . . . oh, it doesn't matter. Where are the others?'

'I lost them,' he said. Once again, he had accepted her presence without question. 'Or they lost me. This mist – I swear it makes you see things. Big, brown things. Astrid, are there bears in this wood too?'

'Oh.'

'"Oh" what?'

'Knut's men – they're berserkers.'

'Berserkers?'

'Wild, landless men – Knut's personal bodyguard. They say that in the heat of battle, berserkers get so out of their minds with bloodlust that they throw off their human shape, and become *real* bears! That's why they're such feared warriors. I've never known whether to believe it – I've never got to see a battle . . .'

'So you think that *they* were the things I saw?'

'It would explain a lot. They live by themselves at a place called Hellir, not far east of Jelling. Too long at home and they get restless, and I'm not let near them.' She wiped the beading mist from her brow. 'Knut will have to take them raiding abroad this summer. He keeps saying he'll go to Ireland, but he's been putting it off these last few years.'

'Why?'

'He wants to be here in case . . . in case anything happens to Father.'

'What sort of thing?'

'Hush!' She clapped a hand to his mouth. Leaning close to his ear, Astrid whispered: 'Don't. Look. Round.'

Instantly he turned, and they both saw.

While they had been talking, six grey wolves had slunk up out of the fog, and were sitting on an outcrop of rock, watching the pair.

ᚾ

'I've got this spear,' said Leif, looking doubtfully down at the shaft in his hands.

'Not much good against six of them, is it?' said Astrid, one eye on him, one on the wolves. Two of them dropped lazily down from the rock, trotting out to either side, red tongues lolling.

Leif raised his spear.

'Leif,' said Astrid, her stomach sinking still further. 'You're pointing it the wrong way round.'

'What kind of wood is it?' he said.

'*What?*'

'The spear. What kind of wood?'

'Um, ash, I think. But –'

'Offspring of the World Tree,' he muttered. 'Kin of Ask and Embla. Giver of the sweet sap and wounding war-needle. Take this, my spark, and fly!'

The haft of the spear burst into flame, and Astrid's eyes bulged. 'How . . . ?'

Leif leapt at the nearest wolf, waving the burning spear like a madman. She had to admire his courage. His technique, not so much.

'You just . . . *ugh* . . . have to speak to things properly, that's all,' he said, as he swung the brand. 'It's nothing special. Take *that*! And *that*! I don't know how the magic works . . . it's never worked *this* well . . .'

He was right. One by one the great grey brutes dropped their heads, turned tail and fled the flame, yowling like puppies. Leif sank back and dropped the spear, which had burnt up almost to his hands. It hissed itself out in the snow.

'I simply try and *understand* a thing – a branch, a stream – and ask it what I want,' he explained, panting. 'And if I'm lucky, then it grants my wish. It works a lot better here at Jelling. I'm sure that you could do it if you tried . . .'

'I –' said Astrid. Then she stopped.

A huge black wolf – surely, the one she'd seen by the river – was hauling itself over the crest of the rocks.

And this time, on its back, one hand grasping the living, hissing snakes that served as the wolf's reins, there rode a witch.

She was grey, naked, hairy, and great tangles of hair coiled round her head. She wore an air of savagery so thick, so primal, that it might have been a cloak about her shoulders. In her wildness, and her fury, she was at once the ugliest and most beautiful thing Astrid had ever seen.

'You,' said Astrid. 'You made the mist!'

How she had been brave enough to speak, she couldn't imagine, but she needn't have bothered. The witch ignored her, extending a taloned finger towards Leif.

'Boy!' she said, with a voice like an eagle's. 'Finally, I find you! I have message.'

'For . . . for me?' he said.

Astrid could only stare.

'Yes, you! It is you who matters.' The witch leered at him, nodding for emphasis. 'It is *you* who will make the choices.'

'Choices?'

'Three choices. The first will be right. The others . . . will be wrong.'

'And is that the message?'

'No! Is just what I can see. Any can see this! Your fate hangs about you like crows on carcass!'

'And why are you *here*?' said Leif.

He was doing this very well, Astrid thought, especially as the witch seemed quite insane.

'Same as you,' said the creature. 'Same as all. I seek power: old power of Yelling Stones. Something comes north, something new. Something very bad. I flee here. We all flee. Only magic of stones can save us.'

'And is *that* the message?'

'*No!*' she shrieked. 'Message is *this*!' And she spat, full in his face, so the spittle splattered his eyes.

Instantly Leif fell to the ground, screaming.

'Not again,' muttered Astrid. He was flailing and frothing just as before, gripped by another fit.

'As for you,' said the witch, at last turning to Astrid.

'Yes?' said Astrid, eager to be part of events.

'Is *no* message! You not matter.'

'Oh,' she said, not sure whether to feel relief or disappointment. 'Well, in that case, I'll just . . .'

'Yes,' cackled the witch, twitching her reins. 'In that case . . . I eat you!'

'Oh,' said Astrid. Well, that settled it: definitely *not* relief. And the black wolf sprang.

SIX

ᚼᚼ

Its heavy front paws bore her to the forest floor, claws rending her cloak. Hot breath, and slobber on her forehead, and she braced herself against the end.

Then came a high, savage cry, and she thought it was the witch. A tremendous blow above, a howl from the wolf, and the weight was off her chest. Astrid rolled to her feet, knife raised, to see the brute scrabbling on the ground, lashing at something in its face. Valvigs her falcon had struck out of nowhere, and its talons were in the wolf's eyes.

The witch lay where she had fallen, slow to rise. Astrid yelled like a mad thing, hurling herself upon the creature, and buried her knife to the hilt in the witch's heart.

She would never forget the feel of the blade sinking deep into flesh, shearing off bone; the weight, the resistance, the slow sag beneath her.

It was done. With an eerie rattle, the witch died, and at once the grey mist lifted. The world was bright and clear again.

Astrid wheeled round, ready to rush to the aid of her falcon.

'I call mine!' It was Knut's voice, and a spear whirred out of nowhere, transfixing the wolf with a dull squelch.

Valvigs flew to Astrid's wrist and she petted his head lovingly. '*All* the mice for you, my love.' She found that her voice was still shaking with the shock of it all.

Knut's men were all around her now, several bearing dead wolves on their burly shoulders. She couldn't help but notice that only Knut carried a spear, and many of the wolves had what looked like claw marks on their pelts.

'That's the last of them, I reckon,' said Knut. 'Curse that mist . . .' Then he saw her.

'Astrid? What are you doing out here?'

'Oh, Knut!' She couldn't help it, but flung herself upon her brother, sobbing hard.

'There there,' he said, bemused. 'What happened, little sister? Was there a witch?'

Dumbly, she nodded.

'And where is it now?'

Astrid looked round. The body had vanished.

'Hey ho,' sighed Knut. 'That's always the way of it. You'd think it wouldn't be too much to ask, just *one* little body to make Haralt eat his words . . .'

Leif screamed again, and Astrid freed herself from Knut's awkward embrace. Wiping her tear-stained face on one torn sleeve, she ran to her friend, remembering how her mother had addressed him last time.

'Speak, Leif,' she said, mimicking Thyre's clear, commanding voice. 'Tell us what you see.'

Just as in the hall, the reply was harsh and grating. 'A green field,' Leif said. 'The sun is low down in the west. Sheep are all around – some white, some black. I move among them, left and right. And now I hear a shepherd's call: he stands before a gate.

'The sheep come trotting in. The first few through the gate are white; he strokes their backs and smiles. A black sheep next – I see a knife – he strikes! The black sheep bleats its last. He has killed it. The same thing happens to sheep after sheep. The white go through unharmed; the black are slain.

'The sun is setting now. And something thrums high up above: the beat of dreadful wings.

'I look down. I myself am black. Am I to be killed like the rest? The awful shepherd's nearer now, and from my throat – a bark! If I'm a dog, then I can save the sheep: can drive them back from that foul gate to where it's safe . . . and dark . . .' His granite voice descended into sobs.

'Awake!' said Astrid, and, for good measure, slapped him hard across the face. Then, repentant, she helped Leif to his feet. He still seemed half asleep.

Knut was scratching his head. 'I wish we had old Bragi here; I'm no good with visions. And it's nothing like the last one he had . . .'

'Both of them had beating wings,' said Astrid. 'And I wonder if the two paths across the river have anything to do with the two sorts of sheep. The witch said Leif had three choices to make, you see – maybe this is one of them.'

'Me, I know what choice I'd make if confronted with a sheep,' said Knut. 'Eat it! All this hunting's gone and made me hungry. Pull yourself together, little poet, and we'll make it back in time for dinner.'

Thyre was livid. 'How *dare* you sneak off, risking life and limb?!' She bore down on Astrid, tall, grim, blue eyes flashing. 'I've never known such foolishness. And after your "adventure" yesterday as well! Well I tell you this, young lady: never again! Henceforth, you will stay at Jelling. You may not stray a bowshot from the hall without my leave, or Knut's, or your father's. And don't even *think* about joining in tonight's feast. Go to your chamber at once!'

Astrid flung herself down on her bed, ears burning. Her mother hadn't been this cross since that time, two years ago, when she had caught Astrid making friends with thralls. At least tonight she'd escaped a whipping . . .

'I'd rather have been whipped,' she thought, 'than shut up in here while the others celebrate.'

Her chest ached where the wolf had struck her, and her eyes were sore from trying not to cry. She snuck a glance at the three other girls, who were being made to keep her 'company'. Bekkhild, Guma and Hyndla sat around moaning, gossiping and weaving, whilst a desultory rain pattered down outside. Doubtless they'd rather Astrid had been whipped as well . . .

And tonight of all nights. This might be the final feast

before all the winter guests returned home, if the snow melted in the rain. More than a hundred men, who had spent the icy months at Gorm's hall, would scatter to their farms and villages. And that meant only one thing: a *really* big party. Even Nisse had abandoned his post, and snuck off to celebrate with his fellow spirits: whole strings of sausages had been known to vanish if you turned your back on nights like these, snatched by the little imps.

Doubtless, Leif was at the centre of the fun, reliving their encounter with the witch and picking over his second vision, which seemed to make him so important in everyone's eyes. Why did *he* get to be the one 'who matters'? She *never* mattered.

All the same, I do like him, she thought. She was still not sure she trusted him. All right, he had twice saved her from wolves. But on the other hand, Leif and the wolves had turned up at the same time . . . And the witch had spoken to him, and left him unharmed. And then again, there were the visions, and the magic he had used to make the spear burn . . .

'I don't trust him,' she decided. 'But he's brave, he's different, and at least he's willing to talk to me.'

The three girls looked round. Then they tittered.

I've finally done it, thought Astrid. *I've started thinking out loud. For the love of Thor, what's wrong with me?* She glowered at the girls until they shut up and went back to their work.

Feeling a little better, Astrid took up her harp. It wouldn't do to just sit here mooning over a boy she didn't even trust.

A simple, handheld thing of oak and catgut, its six strings stretched across a bone bridge, this harp was her one real pleasure throughout the long winter – or, as now, when it rained and she was stuck inside. She sat cross-legged, her left hand cradling the strings from behind, dampening and releasing them as she played.

First, with the nimble fingers of her right hand, she plucked the six open strings almost at random, checking the tuning, scattering a wayward hum of notes across the room. None of the others so much as cocked an ear.

Next, she tried a scale or two, her cold and stiffened fingers warming and unbending to their task. A duff note here, a rogue buzz of string there, but the music was coming. Astrid tossed her head. Then her fingers began to trick up and down, left hand dancing a spider's pattern, tips caressing the backs of the strings, right nails teasing out a succession of chords. Up and down, up and down, rise and fall, the breath of a ghost. She began to work a steady thrum, the progression moving forward, moving back, not yet a tune . . .

Again she glanced up. Still no reaction from her companions. Or – could they be asleep? *All* of them? She kept up the regular, looping lull of notes. Yes – all three were breathing deeply, drooped over their needlework.

Smiling, Astrid forgot the sleepers, forgot everything. Now, above a steady thrum of two low notes, she started to pick out a high, faltering melody. Light, tingling notes fell like droplets upon the room. Unconsciously, her playing had fallen into the rhythm of the rainfall, and now it fell deeper, the tune becoming the rain. She kept returning to one interval – such a sad pairing, the heart-stopping little leap of the tune nestling to the heart of the rain's melancholy . . .

Astrid paused for a moment, to rest her aching fingers. She could hear the revellers nearby, joking and shouting across the hall. But no rain. It had stopped upon the instant.

Frowning, she began again. Knowing full well how foolish it was, she kept one ear out for the sound of renewed rainfall. And it came, matching the time of her playing.

Pure chance, she thought. And besides, the tune was boring her. Raising the tempo, Astrid concentrated on the lower strings, wresting a deeper, fuller sound from the harp.

The rain increased from a shower to a downpour, lashing against the walls of the hall. Hardly daring to believe, Astrid softened her plucking, muting the low string. Instantly, the rain slackened.

She worked the music up again, beginning to add full strums to her picking, and heard an answering rumble from outside. She risked a swift upwards rake of all six strings with her thumbnail. It was met with the crash of lightning. She tried it again. Again the deafening strike, almost directly overhead!

In a sudden fright she flung down the harp, and wrapped her arms around herself. What had Leif said about his magic? 'I simply try and understand a thing . . . I'm sure that you could do it if you tried.'

What if her playing worked like his words?

Then she realised that, though she no longer even held the instrument, the storm still raged. Her three companions were awake, and cowering together in the middle of the room. She listened a while longer. Eventually the din faded back into rain, and then died away altogether. Then began again, a gentle patter.

It was just weather. She was a silly girl, and it had nothing to do with her. Of course it didn't. Of course.

SEVEN

ᛋᛏ�

Astrid woke with the sun, and ran out into a world made new. The storm had sluiced away the snow, and underneath was the true spring. The grass was green enough to make her champ like a horse; bare-washed trees were budding into crisp, free air. Rivulets and trickles ran all around, plashing and pockling like delicate music. Even the Yelling Stones themselves shone wet and clean as river pebbles. It was hard to believe that they could harbour any danger.

Her mood had changed with the weather. Far from begrudging Leif his newfound glory, she wanted to find him, and talk it all over. What were the visions really getting at? What had the witch meant about choices? What was this bad, new something, that was heading north towards them?

And then again, what about the rain, and her harp-playing? She wanted to open out her arms to him and say, 'See this spring? I made this, last night, with my music!'

Just north of the stones rose the low, ancient burial mound

she had pointed out to Leif two nights before. And on the other side of that stood a sacred grove of tall trees. Already, catkins had appeared, fountaining from birches and hazels, and hopeful clusters of purple flowers bloomed upon the Wych elms.

Astrid strolled towards them. She could see a shadow moving among the strangely godlike forms, and was sure it would be Leif.

It wasn't.

'You again?' called Knut. 'Got a taste for trees, eh?'

She cast down her eyes, expecting him to brush past as usual, only to see that he had stopped, and was smiling at her.

'That was brave, what you did yesterday,' he said. 'Just don't let Mother hear I said so!'

She glowed at the unlooked-for praise.

'I tell you what,' he went on. 'Since you're so good with a blade, why not come and help me and Thorbjorn make the sacrifices?'

'Sacrifices – oh, you mean, to give thanks for the end of the winter?'

'That's right – and, more importantly, to gain goodwill for any battles we fight in the coming year!' He rubbed his hands in anticipation. 'We'll be making offerings to Thor, and to Odin.'

'But doesn't Father normally offer the tribute to Odin?' she said.

Knut stiffened. 'Between you and me, sister, he's had a hard winter: we won't see Father up and about so much this year.'

Both were silent for a moment.

'So,' she said at last, eager to keep the mood bright and busy. 'What are we sacrificing?'

'The same for each god – wouldn't want to go offending either of them. It's traditional to offer up the spirits of male animals. Thorbjorn's fetching them now. So that'll be a cockerel for each . . .'

Astrid nodded again. She reckoned she could butcher a cockerel.

'. . . Two rams . . .'

Rams? Just what had she let herself in for?

'. . . And, of course, a pair of oxen!'

She grinned weakly.

Knut was beaming. 'You'll need two things. A knife . . .'

'Got it.' She held up her blade.

'. . . And a bucket.'

'Tell you what,' said Knut, not unkindly. 'From now on, you just concentrate on catching the blood. Thorbjorn and I can handle the other stuff.' Thorbjorn grinned. 'It's what we're best at.'

Astrid wanted to protest – she was up to it, really she was – but the words wouldn't come. She swallowed, hard. *Never again*, she thought, *will I laugh at the expression 'running around like a headless chicken'*. That was two things she'd killed with her knife in two days. How come the cockerel had been so much worse than the witch?

51

But she managed to hold the bucket steady, as Thorbjorn pinned down the struggling white bird, and Knut lopped off the head as casually as if he were top and tailing a carrot.

In fact, Astrid thought, *being a man, he's probably never prepared a carrot in his life.*

At least this time the cockerel lay still, blood weeping from the limp, ridiculous neck.

'Put it down there,' said Knut, and strung up both birds by their legs, just at head height. Astrid placed the bucket beneath them, a little blood falling on her hand as she did so. She pretended to ignore it.

Knut tilted his head to the skies, dropped to one knee, clenched his fists. Holding his left forearm upright in front of his face, he laid his right arm across the top, to make a 'T' – the shape of Thor's hammer. 'I pledge the body of this bird to Thor,' he said.

Then he rose, and mimed the throwing of a spear over the strung-up carcasses. 'And the body of this bird to Odin.'

He looked horrifically embarrassed. Astrid wondered whether the sacrifices were made in private, here in the grove, because it was the custom – or because Knut was afraid to look a fool in front of an audience.

And then all three forgot their pride, and the blood, and the growing hum of insects, as an unmistakable rumble of thunder, and a single clap of lightning, came out of the pure blue sky. Astrid felt the tiny hairs of her neck quiver; her skin prickled all over, as at the touch of a thousand pins.

The gods had accepted their offering. It was all going to be worth it.

Even so, Astrid had a hard time getting through the rams. She tried to think of wide open spaces: seas and skies. She was far, far away, and –

And Knut's sax – a heavy, brutal blade – made a sickening thud as it cleaved through the ram's neck. Blood fountained from the wound, and the poor creature slackened instantly. At least it had been quick . . .

Knut mopped his brow, glancing sidelong at her. Astrid felt sick, and knew it would show, but Knut only shot her a grin, saying to Thorbjorn, 'What courage for a lass, eh? It's not often you find so stout a heart beneath such fine features!'

'She could be the goddess Freyja come again, lord,' said Thorbjorn, and he seemed to mean it.

Astrid felt a bit better after that.

She even stomached the slaughter of the bulls, just about. These – legs trussed together – were secured in turn by the neck to a tree trunk. For this job, Knut had picked up a great, two-handed axe. Quietly, he stepped up behind the ox's shoulder. And then – *ugh*. Trying to ignore the dumb, lowing animals, she focused on the men.

Astrid was tall for her age, but even so Knut towered over her. He was more or less a vast bear, his shaggy brown locks and beard flowing into the furs heaped upon his massive shoulders. He was the only one of Thyre's children not to inherit her straight, golden hair, but, like Astrid, he had her small ears and snub nose, and brilliant blue eyes. The effect of all these little features in so huge a head, atop so big a body, would have been comical, had they not made

53

him even more bear-like. No one would dare laugh at Knut. And Thorbjorn was only a very little smaller.

If Leif's visions do mean there's something bad coming, she thought, *then at least we've the best warriors in the world on our side*.

But then the buzz of flies, and the nightmare stink, brought her mind – and body – back to the task in hand. Astrid paled.

Luckily, they had brought a spare bucket.

:

'When the carcasses have drained,' Knut was saying, 'we'll come back for the blood, and empty the buckets – well, apart from *that* one – into the circle of the Yelling Stones. That's the way it's always been: the bodies for the gods, and the blood for the stones.'

He chuckled. 'You know, it makes me proud to know the gods are pleased. I never thought I'd be any good at this Gothi business, when Father first insisted I take over. Rites and rituals: I've no head for that stuff. But swinging an axe – now that I *can* do!'

The three of them wandered to the well in the courtyard, to wash their hands. And arms. In fact, Astrid noticed, there seemed to be blood *everywhere*.

Teeth chattering at the bite of the near-frozen water, she piped up from between the two men. 'Then why didn't Haralt become the Gothi in Father's stead? It's a big job, that of priest. I'd have thought he'd love all that – the power, the respect, the importance.'

'Between you and me,' said Knut, lowering his voice as far as possible – to something like the level of normal conversation – 'Haralt's never had much time for the gods. He's not Thor's man, like me and Mother, nor Odin's, like Father. And he's such a dry old stick, you can't see him following Frey!'

Astrid blushed, as Thorbjorn sniggered, trying to catch her eye. Frey was the god of fertility, and his worship was not a proper subject for princesses . . .

Knut went on. 'I'm not quite sure Haralt even believes. You heard how he took Leif's story, two nights since. Just yawned, and rolled his eyes. I'm sure he'd dismiss those thunderclaps as just "odd weather".' He said the last words in an affected, squeaky, nasal voice. It *sort* of sounded like their brother.

'Besides,' said Knut, brightening, 'can you see Haralt trying to sacrifice so much as a chicken? Can you even see him *catching* a chicken?'

Even Astrid laughed at this; her second brother's distaste for dirt, and any animal less lordly than a stallion or an eagle, was legendary. Already, the grim reality of the morning was fading, and her heart swelled at the attention.

And that wasn't the end of it. After the mid-morning meal, Knut asked her to help him and Thorbjorn wave off the departing winter guests.

Astrid nearly choked with astonishment. 'But – but wouldn't you rather have Haralt with you? Or Mother? Or even Leif; he's good with words.'

'Our little friend,' said Knut, 'is sleeping off last night's feast. Where he puts it all away, I've no idea, he's so scrawny. But he's paying for it now.'

Astrid raised her eyebrows in what she hoped was a superior sort of manner. 'And Mother?'

'Mother's personally escorting Jarl Tofi back to Baekke. She says he needs sweet-talking. And I must agree that Tofi's getting big for his boots. He thinks he's so grand, with his pure white robe and his close-cropped beard! Really, when will people learn he's just a lily-livered sissy –'

'And Haralt?' said Astrid, interrupting him. She'd heard Knut's views on what made 'real men' too many times before. She loved her brother, but deep down, she suspected Knut's real problems with Jarl Tofi were his wealth, his wit . . . and his way with women.

'Oh, yes, sorry,' said Knut. 'Haralt's taking Grey-cloak and our other nephews off east to Odense, maybe even Lejre, for a week or so. He's never liked these farewells. I'll be bestowing many an arm-ring on our followers as parting gifts, and the sight of all that gold given away makes him sick!'

'It's strange, thinking of Grey-cloak and the rest as our nephews when they're older than you are. Are you even sure we're related?'

'Ach, there's no knowing what Father really got up to before he met Mother; *he's* not telling, that's for sure. Personally, all these names and lineages give me a headache. That's why I need help seeing people off. I don't want to anger anyone by forgetting their father's brother's mother's uncle's name. They'd only start a feud, and then I'd have to kill them – and I've already washed my hands once today!'

By this time, hungover men were mounting horses, and turning north or south along the Ox Road – the ancient, unbroken and shambolic road that ran the length of the land. They would travel back along the Danish peninsular, from the German border in the south, to the seas below Norway in the north. Astrid and the two men hurried to see them on their way.

'Fair riding, Eyvind. I hope the north will meet your taste for trouble!'

'Gods be with you, Knut, and thanks. I'll make sure those Norwegian rat-faces don't dirty the Limfjord!'

'A good wind to you, Ari. May you find your children taller and your wife as plump as when you left them!'

'I pray to Frey she's no fatter! Though your hospitality has taken its toll on me – see how my horse feels its broader burden!'

And so it went on. And on. And on. By the evening, her throat hoarse and her arm sore from waving, Astrid was sick and tired of Knut's boorish jokes and Thorbjorn's raunchy stories. 'They're such boys,' she sighed.

'Not that girls are any better,' she told herself, as she bedded down on her own for the first time in months. Though her three handmaidens had departed with their fathers, their memory – and their smell – would linger here for days. 'In fact, there's only one person around here who's any fun –' closing her eyes – 'At least, he would be –' nodding off – 'if he could learn to hold his food.'

ᚱ

She was sure she'd dream of the strange boy, and it was no surprise to see Leif's shadowed face a hand's span from her own, and to hear his urgent whisper. 'Astrid! There's somewhere we have to go!'

But now she was awake, and he was still there, and it was dark and cold and how had he even got in past the guard, and was that her cloak he was holding?

'Put this on. Follow me.'

Blinking the sleep from her eyes, she did so, creeping past the loose plank in the wall – *her* loose plank – and out into the night. The sudden chill brought her near enough to her senses to spin Leif round and grasp hold of his hair. 'By Sif's sweet mane,' she said. 'Just *what* are we doing out here?!'

'Shh,' he hissed. 'I've had another vision.'

'*Another* one? What happened this time? A talking frog made you king of the mushrooms?'

'Close, but no. Mind your step. I'll explain as we ride.'

'Leif, I've seen you on a horse. You couldn't ride a kitchen stool.'

'That's why we need Hestur. I'll sit behind.'

'You think he'll bear us both?'

'We're very light.'

'All right. The stables are this way. Where are we going, anyway?'

'You'll see.'

'Ow!' She stubbed her foot on a half-sunk stone. 'Leif, let me tell you this much: until tomorrow morning, we're not going to see *anything*.'

58

EIGHT

ᛒᛏᛦ

'In the trance, I was standing by the stones,' he said.

Astrid tried to pay attention, but she couldn't help being more aware of his cheek against hers, his arms around her waist, as she guided Hestur down the narrow, starlit track that led south from Jelling, down to Lake Faarup.

'I heard a yell – but not the stones, you see – and found a falcon staring in my eyes. It cried again, a cry to break your heart, and led me south for ages, into the fens. I picked my way among the marsh, to where a place was marked with scorched and blackened trees. I'd know my way again, it was so clear.'

'And then?'

'I saw . . . something. At this point it gets all confused; I only know I've got to go and see it in the real world, right away.'

Trees closed overhead, shutting out the stars, the track becoming a tunnel through the wood. Astrid tried to control her temper. She failed. 'So we're wandering alone, at night, on one horse, headed into the *fens*, looking for something you saw in a trance? Leif, in case you've forgotten, I've been forbidden from having any more of these little adventures. You know, because of those two times we *nearly died*?'

'We didn't, though, did we? Still, if you're scared . . .'

'Scared? Who's talking about scared? I'm sane, that's what I am. Sane.'

'Come now; don't tell me you're not having fun.'

As they picked their way down rocky gullies, neither knew it, but both of them were smiling, in the dark.

ᚾ

'What was that?! Was it a dis?'

'That, Leif, was an owl.'

'Oh.'

For all his talk of her being scared, Leif was remarkably jumpy every time the night made a noise. Disir, landvaetter, draugurs – there was almost no sort of spirit he hadn't thought he'd heard. It came of growing up underground, she supposed. Now a low, eerie warble came from away to their left. 'Wow wow wow,' it went.

'A witch!'

'A fox. I'd have thought you'd recognise a fox.'

'Well, I was just a baby at the time.' He paused. 'So, tell me about that lake on our right. I could do with taking my mind off things.'

'That's Lake Faarup,' she said. 'It's pretty huge, and full of all sorts of creatures.'

'Then why didn't we pass any houses? Surely there'd be fishermen living there.'

'I said "creatures", not fish. Being so close to the Yelling Stones has taken its toll on the waters: you hear stories of all manner of monsters. It's even said – well, Bragi always said – that the bottom of the lake leads straight to Hel, and if you could only hold your breath long enough, you could swim all the way down to the underworld!'

She thought for a moment. 'Or, I suppose, something else could swim all the way *up*.'

'I really wish,' Leif said, 'I hadn't asked.'

†

The night deepened. They were now far from the haunts that Astrid knew; this southern path, though the shorter route to the farming villages of Vorbasse, Baekke and the south, was rarely used, since it cut through bogs that were perilous even by day. She hoped Leif's vision had been an accurate one. The night was clear, but the moon was new, and they had only the stars' faint glimmerings to go by.

Already, she could feel the ground softening beneath Hestur's hoofs; they jolted less and less, and had slowed to little more than a walk. And as the familiar black presence of the trees fell away, replaced by whispering rushes and straggling gorse, even Astrid had to admit that the night calls around them were distinctly weird. No longer could she say 'badger' or 'nightjar' with anything like confidence. The wails and shrieks they now heard really did sound otherworldly.

For a long time, neither spoke. Just once, Leif broke their silence. 'You see that patch of bog that's on our right? It's odd, in all this black, how it can be *so* black – far darker than the night. It's like the earth has mouths . . . I'll shut up now.'

'I wish you hadn't said that,' said Astrid. Now, every opening of the mere around them felt like a sucking, darkling mouth, ready to drink them in with one sinister squelch. If there were witches in the woods, what worse things might there be here, in this wild place of reeds and vapours?

She began to see eyes in the darkness, too large, or too odd in number, to be those of animals. At one point she could have sworn she heard a cackling, from directly behind them, going on and on. But she was not going to look round, not on her life. And then, a little later, there were lights bobbing over blackness, from off to their left. Neither was so foolish as to even mention them.

Surely, she thought. *Surely, we must be nearly there?*

'Stop!' said Leif. 'I think I see the place.'

Hestur halted gladly enough. Leif gestured vainly in the dark, then laid a hand on Astrid's head and turned it to the right. 'See there?' he said. 'That clump of wizened trees. They block out half the stars. It's off the path.'

'We'll have to dismount,' she said, and did so. A tumble and an oath told her that Leif, too, had got down – after his own fashion. She helped him up. His hand in hers was sticky and slippery with the muck of the fens.

'That's definitely the place you saw?'

'Those are the trees, see? Three of them. Bare, dead, forking into the sky. Yes, it's the place.'

'I make it four trees. At least . . . Leif, do you feel a wind? Surely that tree's too big to be rocking like that.'

'I see five trees now. No, six. That one rose up out of the ground, I'm sure of it!'

'Leif?'

'Astrid?'

'I don't think those are trees.'

'Astrid, let's run.'

They turned to where Hestur had stood a moment ago, but he was already bolting, back along the path he had trod so gingerly before. The pair wheeled back round, and froze. Looming high above them, a living mass of black against black sky, were three –

'Trolls,' breathed Astrid. 'They're trolls.'

NINE

ᚻᛁᚲ

Before Leif could open his mouth in reply, the night fell on them. Astrid felt the marsh embrace her, and then – and then oh such a dizzying rush of up and up and the thick black glooping, the suffocation, all dank and death and oozing pitch. She made to scream, and the bog was in her mouth and up her nose and how had her ribs not cracked –

And then the earth unfolded, open skies around again. Astrid peeled open her eyes, lids thick with the heavy, cold slime, and met a giant's gaze: two huge troll eyes, sunk deep inside a craggy face, regarding her, unblinking.

She was standing, she thought, on a wet peat tussock, matted with sedge – but standing high in the air. From behind, she heard a sucking sound, and turned to see Leif rising once more to his feet, clambering towards her over what might have been four huge, half-sunken logs of bog-oak. She could have screamed again at the sight of him, for Leif was completely covered in mud, at one with the mere – as she must be herself, she thought.

She turned again, back to those pooling eyes. *We must be standing on the troll's hand.*

'Now might be the time for you to talk to them,' she whispered to Leif.

She heard him gulp – she felt him tremble – but somehow, somehow he found his tongue.

'Peace be on you and yours,
Jotunn of the marshes.
Swallower of sky-wheel,
Seek not to cause us harm.'

Well, thought Astrid, *they haven't eaten us yet.*

'Warden of the wetlands,
We've come to give you aid.
Sent by sleep-sights, we rode;
Sought out your fell abode.'

He stopped, teeth knocking together, quivering all over and shedding lumps of bog with every twitch. Astrid waited for something to happen.

For a time, nothing. *Come on*, she thought. And then: *No! I take it back!* – for the troll's mouth had opened.

That terrible maw was the size of the Great Hall doors; a foul cave filled with broken, stony teeth, livid sores raised on its gums. It was dark, but she thought she saw things moving in there: small creatures crawling over and between the vicious teeth. Frogs? Snakes?

Somewhere in the cave-dark, a glistening, globbing tongue stirred. And, unbelievably, the troll spoke.

'Do I smell the wound-sweat
Of sons of ash and elm?

Tell me, tiny manlings,

Truth to save your brain-walls.'

Astrid could just make out the words – low, slow; all mulching and golloping. As far as she could follow, they were being told to speak up – or else . . .

She nudged Leif, urging him to reply, but he just swayed a little. She suspected he was about to faint.

The troll rumbled angrily.

'Faster, foes of troll-kin!

For we've had much grief here.

I long to rend and lap,

Lunch upon bone marrow!'

There was nothing for it: Astrid had to say something. 'Um, fair . . . well . . . troll. Sorry, I'm no good at this. But it's true, what he said. We've come all the way out here, from Jelling, because of something he saw in a trance. He has these . . . these visions, you see. And this one told him to come here, right now. A falcon led him. He didn't tell me any more . . .'

She glanced at Leif, in time to see him flop over on the troll's palm. He *had* fainted.

'We know about the boy,' said the first troll. 'Brought news, we were, of him. "Here's hope," came the message. "He'll maybe solve this wrong."'

Astrid's heart sank as she realised the troll would only speak in poems. But she dredged up the courage to ask: 'What wrong?'

For answer, the troll turned. Astrid lurched at the sudden rush, tumbling down to land beside Leif and fearing they would both fall further. But those hoary, bog-oak fingers curled up and cupped them gently, then set them down on the ground. Astrid leapt aside as Leif rolled past her, plopping into the fetid water. To judge by the noise he was making, this at least woke him back up. But Astrid had no time for him now. She saw what the troll had meant.

Beneath the blasted trees lay a long, hulking, low shape that at first she took for a hall, roofed with turf. Or it might have been a whale, beached absurdly far inland and weltered all over with seaweed and barnacles. Or, the fallen mother of all trees.

But of course, it was none of these things. It was a troll, dying.

'Astrid?' said Leif, in a vole-sized voice. 'Astrid, do you think that we can help it?'

A moan came from the felled troll then, sad enough to break her heart, and deep enough to break rocks. This morning's sacrifices had been nothing, she realised: if a *hundred* bulls had lowed a lament, it would not have come close to this.

'Aurnir, my eldest son,' said the troll. 'A handsome lad, he was. But now he's faced the beast; brought low with a death-hurt.'

Now Astrid could make out his head, his limbs, his chest, and saw the awful gash across his side. The wound was deep, and raw, and out from his innards there welled a tarry substance that must have been his blood.

'That was some blow, to bring down a troll,' she breathed. 'See the edges of it, too? They're almost charred . . .'

In fact, she now saw what must have been burns all over its body. But she thought better of mentioning this to Leif: he'd fainted once already. So she looked instead at its pain-wracked face. Its eyes were closed; it clearly had no idea they were there. It wouldn't be long now.

'What could have caused this kind of harm?' said Leif.

The troll-mother was sobbing now, and a small waterfall of mud and slime began to fall. Swiftly, the two of them stepped back, as she tried to reply.

'It hailed from the hawk-land,
High and grim and shining.
It brought the bright hall-wolf,
Bad thiever of forests.

'Its fast battle-fire
Fell swift on my Aurnir;
A flurry of wind-oars
Overcame his attacks.'

'I'm sorry,' said Astrid, 'but I just don't understand. What kind of man, or . . . or monster . . .'

But it was no use. Grief overwhelmed the giant creature, and she staggered back into the arms of the other two trolls. Tremors rocked them where they stood.

The sorrow-stricken troll made one last attempt at speech.

'My Svadi and Svarang
Support me as I fall.
But they cannot thwart this,

68

These last of my children.
I fear for my two sons;
Fierce is the bright slayer.
We look to you, thumblings,
To halt its . . . its . . .'
Her final words were drowned in a wild howling. Instantly, her sons joined in, inconsolable as babies and unstoppable as a storm. The trolls began beating their breasts, stamping the unstable earth in their total despair.

Leif stood his ground. 'We *will* help you, and stop what caused this hurt,' he managed to say. Then Astrid seized his arm and tugged him aside, as a colossal foot descended. 'Run!'

And they ran.

TEN

ᛏᛁᚾ

As soon as they were well clear of the demented trolls –
and, incredibly, back on the path – the pair slowed to a
gasping, gulping halt. In the distance, the mayhem continued,
sounding like a series of small eruptions, sending whole
flocks of waterfowl flying.

Leif was panting, eyes wild. 'Trolls! Oh, Astrid! I've never
been so scared . . .'

Astrid stared at him. 'I can see that,' she said. 'I'd have
thought, being raised by dwarfs, you'd be more prepared
for something like this.'

'Oh Hel, Astrid, there never were any dwarfs! Come on;
let's get out of here.'

'Oh, you're not going anywhere!' She was seriously cross
now. 'Not till you explain what you just said.'

'Not right now, it's not the time –'

'Leif, it's the perfect time. We're alone. It's still dark. We've
got a *lot* of walking to do. And if you don't start telling the

truth – the whole truth – well, there's no one to see me bury you in this bog. I'll do it. I swear I will!'

'Oh, I believe you.' He was still struggling for breath, doubled up, hands on knees. 'I made a mistake, I can see that now. I should have told you, Astrid. And I will. But promise me that this goes no further?'

She softened. They'd both just come through the fright of their lives, after all. 'You, me and the fen. No further,' she promised.

'Then I'll tell you.' Slowly, shakily, the two began to pick their way northwards, and Astrid listened, as Leif told, once more, the story of his life.

ᛁ

'Since I was born, I've lived in Hedeby. I never knew my father, just his name: he came from foreign parts, and soon moved on. He was a Jew, or a Muslim, I think – one of those ones who can't eat pork, you know? My mother died in giving birth to me; *her* father died for Gnupa in the war against the Saxons, many years ago.'

'Hedeby!' Astrid let out a whistle. Hedeby was the richest town in Gorm's kingdom, far down on the east coast, right by the German border. Gorm had defeated the young King Sigtrygg of Hedeby, son of this Gnupa, some six years before she was born, and now the place was a magnet for traders from across the whole world. She'd often longed to see it.

Hedeby, in other words, was about as much like a dwarven cave, as the moon was like a duck.

'I'm sorry to hear about your family,' she said. 'But oh, I could so punch your face right now!'

'Do you want to hear my story or not?'

She had no answer to this.

'So, then: my mother's father was a Dane. My mother's *mother* was a Finn, who brought me up alone. She taught me all I know. She must have had some magic in her blood, and got by as a healer . . . and a witch. From her, I learnt of runes, and charms, and gods. She was a fine poet in her own right, though no one wished to hear a woman's words.'

'Don't I just know it,' Astrid muttered.

'She loved me very much, and made a plan that, once she was no more, I'd come up north to earn my keep and win my name with Gorm. That story, with the fox and dwarfs, was hers: she thought that it would help to get me in. And, of course, explain away my dark skin . . . This plan – for my success – was all she had.'

'But – hang on – if there were no dwarfs, then what about that sword? Even Weland's never seen its like.'

'My father left it, out of guilt, I think. It comes from Toledo, a city in the south; they call those letters "Arabic". My grandmother told me I could go far with such a sword – but not by wielding it.'

'I can believe all this,' said Astrid, after a long pause. 'I mean, I only half believed your last story: this is all far more convincing. But I still don't know where I am with you. The visions, the magic . . .'

Anger was rising within her again like the uncoiling of a serpent. 'And now I've heard both a troll and a witch say

72

they recognise you, and that you're, I don't know, *fated* to make mysterious choices and avert some great danger. Just who are you, Leif? Who the Hel are you?'

'I'm *Leif*. Just Leif. And, so I thought, your friend.'

She could tell she'd really hurt him this time, and tried to speak, but Leif went on. 'You think I *want* to roll round on the floor? To be suspected by my only friend? I've no idea where those things came from. I didn't ask for them, I didn't want . . .'

He took a deep breath, trying to control himself. 'I hadn't planned to get lost in a bog, or stomped by trolls, or any of those things. I'm just a town boy, not used to the wilds. And Jelling's not like home. The stones, the trees – the whole place hums with magic! If I knew I'd get these trances, then I'd never have come. The plan was simple, and it would have worked. But ever since that night, back in the gorge, so many things – odd things – it's all so *hard* . . .' He turned his face away.

'All right, all right! No need to cry.' She paused. Tried to be more helpful. 'Though, if you wanted to cry, I wouldn't be able to tell. It's dark; you're covered in slime anyway. Just so you know.'

'Thanks,' he said, wetly.

Astrid was beginning to brighten. 'I suppose, if all you wanted was an easy life, arm-rings from the king and a good spot on the bench, it must seem more than you bargained for. But isn't it *exciting*? All this dark foreboding, I mean. Jelling's always been a strange place, but this is something else! Omens, trolls, some mysterious "beast" on the loose.

It's just like in *Beowulf*!'

'Yes, all those things,' he said. 'And then . . . there's *you*.'

'Me? What do you mean, me?'

'Oh, Astrid. Astrid . . . Tell you what; forget that I said that. But please . . . Astrid . . . trust me?'

'All right,' said Astrid. 'All right. I trust you.'

ELEVEN

ᛁᛗᚦᛁ

The wan light of before-dawn found them stumbling along the half-there path: two sodden, spattered figures, clutching each other for support, still sinking in bog up to their knees whenever they put a foot wrong.

A remorseful whinny broke in on their torment.

Astrid raised her head. 'Oh, there you are, Hestur.' Her voice was dull, empty of surprise. Already half asleep, they groped their way onto his back, and he began the long walk homewards.

ᚠ

Slumped against Astrid, arms around her, gently bobbing on Hestur's back, Leif began to feel the pull of heavy magic. 'No,' he twitched. He didn't want any of that. No prophecies, no visions. He had never been so content in all his life as at that moment: trusted, and tired, and just where he wanted to be. But that place – caught between waking and sleeping – was a dangerous one, where the otherworld was always near, and strange things skulked in the shadows of dreams.

↓

Astrid felt the boy's whole body stiffen at her back, and wriggled closer down on Hestur's neck. She was deep in a dream of her own. It was all about sausages.

⋮

The world was grey, pale, ghastly, streaked with the glimmering of dawn. Leif could tell that something had shifted, somewhere, and the hackles rose on his neck. 'Is anything . . . is anybody there?' he whispered.

Silence. Just the steady, squelchy clop of Hestur's hoofs.

And then the horse turned its heavy head, to look him full in the face, and its eye was made of stone.

Leif almost fell from its back, digging in at the last moment with heel and nails to keep his seat. Hestur, normally so flighty, walked on as if nothing were happening. But that dead, baleful, stony eye remained fixed on Leif.

'What are you?' said Leif, his voice low. It was crazy, talking to a horse – but then, after the trolls, he was ready to believe anything.

Hestur's mouth barely moved, a rasping, sibilant hiss all that escaped the large, yellow teeth. '*We are sisters; we are stone*,' came the hiss.

'The Yelling Stones?'

'*The same. Three visions we have sent you; now we use this vessel.*'

'*You* sent me the visions? Then, why speak now?'

'*The time for games is at an end: the blood begins to run. A danger comes to Jelling that may spell the end for all.*'

'The beast? This thing that killed the troll, you mean?'

'*Something bigger. Something new. This beast is but its weapon. It comes to kill our kin – troll, witch, dis, dwarf – and to steal our power. We look to you, small one, to find out what it is.*'

'To me?'

'*We are stone; still; lifeless. You are flesh, you are blood and bone, speed and skill. Find this thing out. Before it is too late.*'

'I swore already I would help the trolls. But why choose me? Jelling has its heroes . . .'

The hiss redoubled, venomous, bitter. '*Seek help from those followers of Thor and of Odin? Those who slay wolves and witches? Never! Your skin is dark. You are raised in word and magic. You do not belong with these proud, pale Danes. What better champion could we choose?*'

Leif was stung. 'Well, and what *of* Odin?' he retorted. 'Are the gods of no use in this battle?'

'*Odin and the rest take shelter within Asgard's walls and wait for Ragnarok, the end of the world; only his two ravens stray about the earth. And the beat of their wings has not been felt at Jelling for many ages. They are too blind to see what all our kin can sense: this is the battle that needs fighting, here and now. If you fail us, then the old world falls, and Ragnarok will never come to pass.'*

For a long time, Leif was mute, struggling to take this in. 'You . . . you want me to save the world from *not* being destroyed?' he managed, at last.

The hiss changed, almost a laugh – the wretched, wheezing cackling of crones. Hestur's unsuspecting mouth contorted to a rictus grin, lips drawn back obscenely. Leif sensed the strength of the magic fading; could see the stony eye crumbling into dust.

'Wait!' he said. 'There's more I have to know. The other witch, the one that rode the wolf, she said that I have to make three choices . . .'

But the eye that blinked back at him was wet, brown, stupid. Hestur turned his head away with a shiver and a whinny; Astrid stirred and mumbled. That uncanny presence had withdrawn, leaving a boy, a girl and a horse, alone upon the earth.

TWELVE

ᛏᚻᚠ

'*I* think it's a dragon,' said Astrid, and then, 'Pass me the soap.'

They had slipped through Jelling unseen – it was still early – and crept into the privacy of the steaming bathhouse to get clean.

Leif recounted his conversation with the stones as best he could. He seemed distracted by something, and kept looking at a bare patch of wall.

Astrid had no idea why: all she was doing was having a good scrub . . .

'Not a dragon. The stones said "something new",' said Leif.

'They weren't exactly helpful,' Astrid said. 'And I mean, they're only stones. They're just as much in the dark as we are.'

'I wish the troll-mother had been clearer,' Leif said.

'Well, poems are your lookout, after all. Towel?'

He handed it to her, averting his eyes. 'Um . . . yes . . . I mean . . . I mean, let's think. How did she put it?'

79

He was bright red, she noticed. And they weren't even in the steam room yet.

'Your turn to wash,' said Astrid, dropping the towel to the floor as she moved towards the sauna. Leif, overcome, leapt back – onto the soap – and pitched, fully clothed, into the cold pool.

:

Side by side in the sauna, it was Astrid who had to remember most of the troll's poem. Leif, clinging to the towel and staring at his feet, was still having trouble concentrating.

'So,' she said, 'if we're going to go out searching for this beast, we need to work out what the troll-mother meant. So far we've remembered:

'It hailed from the hawk-land,
High and grim and shining.
It brought the bright hall-wolf,
Bad thiever of forests.

'Its fast battle-fire
Fell swift on my Aurnir,
A flurry of wind-oars
Overcame his attacks.'

'Well,' she went on, 'the hawk-land is obviously the sky, even I can tell that, so of course it was "high". What about "shining"?'

'Those next two lines just mean "fire",' said Leif.

'Then why say "fast battle-fire" as well? Stupid troll . . .'

'No,' said Leif, 'I think that one means "sword". And "wind-oars" are wings. Well, we knew that.'

'So: the beast came from the sky, with fire, and attacked Aurnir with a sword. And its wings. Hmm,' said Astrid. 'The question is, how much do we rely on the poetic ravings of a half-mad troll. I'll repeat that: *troll*.'

'If it weren't for the wings, she might have been describing a lightning bolt,' said Leif. 'You saw the blasted trees. It all makes sense.'

'And the . . . the body . . . It was definitely burnt.'

'Maybe the wings were poetic licence? But then, they came into all my visions . . .'

'I'm still saying dragon,' said Astrid. 'That wouldn't be so bad. Imagine how happy it would make Knut, getting to fight a dragon!'

'We can't tell Knut of this, nor your parents,' said Leif. 'The stones said they would never ask their help.' No; they had chosen *him* as their champion. His chest swelled secretly at the thought. 'You're always saying how you're overlooked,' he pointed out. 'This is our chance to prove ourselves, Astrid.'

'Oh, I'm ready for the fight, if you are,' she said. 'And what's more, I can prove it!'

Leif gulped when he saw what was in her hand, and he remembered the traditional ending to a sauna . . . 'Ow! Astrid, put those birch twigs down! Astrid!'

They emerged, blinking at the sunlight, to the blare of horns and the thud of many hoofs.

Astrid paused. 'We can't present ourselves like this,' she said. 'At least, I can't.' They were loosely robed in thin linen shifts.

'If something's happening, I want to watch,' said Leif, and tugged her after him. Together they scampered to the shadowed side of the hall, flattening themselves against the smooth wooden posts that slanted down from the outer wall. From here, they could see it all.

A swirl of horsemen poured from the road into the space before the hall doors. First among them, flanked by his Norwegian nephews, was Haralt. He wore a fine white tunic, edged with beaver, that Astrid had not seen before. 'Maybe Jarl Tofi's started a new fashion,' she smirked.

Haralt reined in his mount, calling for grooms, his sparse blond beard glinting on his jutted-out chin in the brilliant morning light. The din of a dozen flapping cloaks crowded with the sound of restless hoofs, breaking up the clean and quiet air.

Behind the riders, a wagon yawed into the yard. There was something odd about it, and Astrid scrunched her eyes up against the sun to make it out. The cart was a simple, rickety affair – nothing she hadn't seen before – except that above it flew a yellow banner emblazoned with a black, two-headed eagle, wings spread. Below the banner stood a high wooden cross.

The wagon slewed to a halt behind the horsemen, and again, the horns brayed out. By now, a large crowd had gathered, and the pair had to crane their necks to see past them.

The hall's high doors creaked apart, and Knut strode out, all furs and helm and gold around his arms. 'What news, brother?' he called. 'What brings you back so soon, and in such a clamour? Some of us, lustier for the yeast-sea than you, have sore heads to stand such tootings!'

Haralt slid from his saddle. 'Where's Father? I've a guest to greet him; we met his ship on the way to Odense.'

'Within,' growled Knut. 'Will this guest not see me first?'

The horns sounded again, more cautiously this time, and a man descended from the wagon as an avalanche descends a mountain.

'You're *enormous*,' whispered Astrid, as she had before the wolf.

He was a real whale of a man, and his robes were black waves, flowing over and around his massive girth as he lumbered towards Knut.

If Knut is a like a bear, then he's *a boar*, thought Leif. The man's short black hair bristled out from beneath the top of his robes, creeping over mighty folds of neck to circle a bald head. He had no beard. Just small, dark eyes sunk deep in wobbling cheeks.

He's got sausages for fingers, thought Astrid. The stubby digits of his left hand gripped a gilded crook, its wicked metal point scoring the soft spring earth.

The man juddered to a halt before Knut, spread his arms,

and slowly passed his pudgy right hand back and forth across his body.

Knut took half a step backwards, and they could see how hard his own hands were clenched. A spasm flicked over his face.

'This is Bishop Folkmar, emissary of Otto, King of Germany,' said Haralt. 'And he's come to speak to the king.'

THIRTEEN

ᚦᚱᛁᛏᛖᚾ

Once more, the hall was thronged with watchers – women too – as Gorm sat in council. But the mood was changed entirely from the evening Astrid had brought Leif back to court. Shafts of light, thick with circling dust, pierced the walls like arrows; the air was free from smoke; most of the benches remained empty. The king's men had all left for their homes the day before, and the only warriors left were Knut's berserkers, ranged along one side, and Haralt's Norwegian bondsmen, sat across from them. The space above their heads was still – Astrid sensed that the hall-spirits were keeping well out of the way of this new visitor.

Leif now had one of the best seats in the hall, and Astrid sat with him where Arinbjorn the Unlucky would have been, except that the old Norwegian had shifted sides to be with his kinsmen. Her father and brothers alone sat in state upon the dais; the bishop had the floor. He fairly filled the high hall with his bulk, and his presence.

'Greetings to you, Saxon,' said Gorm, and his thin cold voice sent a breath of winter through that airy place. 'What brings one of Otto's liegemen to my realm?'

'Majesty, I am arrived here at your palace, to endow you and all your subjects with the gift most precious that may be bestowed.'

Astrid was surprised by how deep and rich the foreigner's voice was. She had assumed he would sound, as well as look, like a pig.

'You speak of gifts,' said Gorm. 'Lately, I was brought a worthy gift indeed –' and he smiled in Leif's direction – 'and even when an old man feels the call of the grave, a fine thing to take to Odin's hall is always welcome. Let us see what you have brought.'

The bishop beamed, and Gorm leant forward in his eagerness. Even Astrid was curious: the wealth of Christ-men was well known, while the wealth of the Saxon king was the stuff of legend.

Folkmar swept his crook high in the air. He seemed to be gesturing to the narrow shafts of sunshine. 'Your Majesty, what I bring you is the light. The light of the world, and of the Word! I am giving to you . . . salvation!'

'Ah,' said Gorm. 'I was hoping for an axe, you know?'

†

The hall was split. As soon as they understood the priest's proposal, Knut's berserkers began to growl. Weland, sitting to Astrid's right, hawked up a great gob of phlegm which he

86

spat across the dusty floor. She shuffled as far as she could to her left without actually ending up in Leif's lap. But on the far side of the fireplaces, Haralt's men were whispering earnestly.

At the high table, Gorm and his two sons threw the idea back and forth like dogs worrying a bone.

'This must be what the little skald's visions were warning us about,' said Knut. 'Even I can work that one out: we've a choice to make, between Christ and the old gods. And in my mind, it's no choice at all. I'm too heavy to walk on water, and I don't much fancy being one of those slaughtered black sheep – bah!'

'I knew this day would come without omens,' said Gorm. 'Ever since the old man at Hamburg named those three Christ-men to rule in my towns. *My* towns! If they'd dared to show up, I'd have shown them who rules the Danes!'

'But Folkmar isn't *from* Hamburg,' said Haralt. 'He stands well at Otto's court. We would be wise to win his friendship, or the next time he makes this offer, it might come on the point of a German spear.'

'It's happened before, you know,' said Gorm. 'You won't remember it – it was the year you got your first teeth, Knut – but this isn't the first time one of these bishops has come a-begging. Unni, the last one was called, and no comfort did he find in my hall.'

'I say we send the fat man packing,' said Knut.

'He is a guest,' retorted Haralt. 'And we should hear him out.'

'Oh, you follow what god you wish, little brother! I am

for Thor and always will be. Father follows Odin. If this Christ can reward your allegiance, I've no quarrel with your choosing him. Just don't start nagging me not to eat horse, that's all I ask.'

'It's not a personal matter, Knut, this is political . . .'

'Hah, hear what I said? "Nagging me not to eat horse" – maybe I'll be a poet yet . . .'

At the words, 'this is political', Astrid stopped listening, fixing her attention on the priest. Folkmar, she saw, had not so much as blinked, but stood, massive and somehow inevitable, waiting at the centre of the hall.

Leif nudged her. Her brothers' bickering was coming to a close.

'Well, he's not staying in our room,' Knut was saying.

'Give him our sister's bed,' said Haralt. Now Astrid really started listening. 'She can sleep in the stables: the guests' horses are gone and the stalls stand empty.'

Astrid had just opened her mouth to object, when Gorm rose to his feet. 'Quiet,' he barked, like a grizzled old wolf. 'Bishop, you are welcome to stay with us, and we will debate this matter further at our ease, in the days to come. There may be something in what you say. He who acts swiftly in battle may save his life, but he who bargains with his *next* life cannot afford to be so rash. This meeting is over.' And, with a rueful glance at Thyre's empty chair, the king melted back into his usual darkness.

Folkmar bowed his head, turned, and waddled from the hall.

The room emptied, Leif and Astrid among the last out.

People were streaming past on either side, chattering or quarrelling. But Folkmar, they noticed, had come to a halt, ignoring the excited Danes.

He was staring fixedly, with a look of such hunger and resolve on his piggy features that Astrid shrank back, her skin crawling.

She noticed his free hand – the one not holding the golden crook – rapidly opening and closing, as it hung at his side. Each time the fat fingers made a fist they squeezed, as if cracking a nut.

She looked back up; followed his gaze.

Folkmar was staring – where else? – at the Yelling Stones.

And now she remembered where she'd seen that look before: on Leif's face, that first night they had talked about the stones.

So she wasn't surprised when Leif put his mouth to her ear and whispered. 'I think our "something new" has just arrived.'

FOURTEEN

ᚠᛁᚾᚱ

'I still don't see why I have to do this.' Leif raised his left arm to wipe his brow, unthinking.

'No, Leif, don't – oh, never mind,' said Astrid, and watched, as he hit himself in the face with his large, wooden shield.

They were in the sacred grove, out of sight of the hall, and – she had made sure of this – upwind of where the grisly sacrifices still swung. Here, the air was heady with the scent of trees in leaf: a dizzy waft of bark and flower and catkin. Both had a shield strapped to their left arm. In their right hands, they held blunt wooden swords.

'Don't make me go over it again,' Astrid said, as Leif rubbed his swelling forehead. 'And take your guard. No – like I showed you – left knee forward, shield out, sword raised over your right shoulder. Facing forward. No – with the *point* forward, Leif, like a horn, that's why it's called the ox guard . . .'

Pity and fascination fought for control of her features as she watched him try to get it right. 'We're doing this,' she reminded him, 'for practice. In case we have to fight the beast.' They'd worked it all out. If Folkmar was the new power that had come to Jelling – and what else could he be? – then it stood to reason that he was the one controlling the beast that had killed the troll. Christian priest-craft was one of the strongest sorts of magic – even she knew that.

And it wasn't only the troll: shepherds and farmers were telling tales of all sorts of weird creatures and spirits, found dead in the fields and forests around Jelling. Spirits of trees, spirits of rocks, found dead, their bodies slashed and burnt. The Danes saw these beings as guardians who gave them luck, and the sudden spate of killings had everyone worried. Everyone, of course, except Folkmar . . . and Haralt.

'But we can't prove that Folkmar is the one behind the beast,' Astrid said again, taking up an identical guard to Leif's, only without all the wobbling. 'And we'll need proof if we want to stop him. Now: shield up!'

In slow motion, she stepped forward with her right foot, thrusting her wooden sword at Leif's unprotected head.

Scowling, he raised his shield just in time to block. 'I still think we should just spy on the priest,' he said.

'Switch legs and cut!' she ordered, pulling out of the attack and swinging her sword low all in one slow movement, aiming at his exposed left knee. 'But the beast clearly isn't with him,' she said. 'So we'll have to go looking for it.'

Leif executed an awkward hop on the spot, throwing his left leg back out of danger and leading with his right. He grinned with pride. 'I did it!'

'You forgot the cut,' she said. 'You must cut at my head as you switch legs. Lesson number one: practice makes perfect. We'll have to start again . . .'

'But if the beast's a dragon, as you say,' he objected, 'I don't think it'll *use* a sword and shield.'

The problem, as Astrid saw it, was this. Leif's idea of action was sticking close to Folkmar, listening in dark corners, waiting for him to let something slip. Whereas the very thought of being stuck in an enclosed space anywhere near that revolting man brought her out in a cold sweat. Action, to her, meant exploring. Hunting. Fighting. And doing it outside, where sunshine dappled their skin beneath branches, birds sung, and fallen oak leaves and soft pine needles rustled underfoot.

That was why she was trying to teach Leif the basics of swordplay.

'Never hurts to be prepared,' she said. 'We'll go over it once more – full speed this time.'

Still grumbling, Leif took up the position.

She thrust – he parried – slipped – she shifted her swing, thwacking the flat of the wooden blade hard against his exposed behind.

'Ow!' he yelled, and dropped his sword.

'That's known as a "shaming-stroke",' she said. 'If you were a real warrior, you'd be dishonoured for letting me do that.'

'It's lucky for us both, then, that I'm not,' he said, rubbing his bottom. 'That warrior stuff's all stupid anyway.'

'Some of the greatest skalds have been legendary fighters,' she said. 'Your hero Egil Skallagrimsson for one.'

'True. But he was also three times my size,' Leif pointed out. 'If you want to fight, I'll do things *my* way.'

'All right,' she said. 'What're you going to do, talk to my shield and make it burn?'

'There's more than fire to my magic,' he said. 'On guard!'

Intrigued, she raised her sword. Only, it wasn't a sword any more . . .

'Hear the sun and soil call: shrug off your man's shaping,' said Leif.

Astrid found that she was holding a flowering shrub in each hand. Laughing, she threw them aside.

'Lesson number two,' she said. 'Always improvise!'

Leif yelled, as Astrid dived for his legs, sending them both rolling on the springy, moss-grown forest floor. With a cry of triumph, she kneeled over him – pinned his arms – his face so close that she could feel his breath, hot and ragged on her cheeks . . .

There was a cough, close at hand. They looked up.

Standing, arms folded, beneath the foamy spread of a new-budding linden, flanked by slender birches, one eyebrow raised impossibly high . . . was Queen Thyre.

Astrid gulped. 'Hello, Mother,' she said.

ᚦ

'The time for play is at an end,' said Thyre. 'Get up.'

They scrambled to their feet, dusting twigs and blossom from their clothes. For the first time, Leif noticed the queen's height, the way she held her head, and how much she looked like all that was strong in her three children.

'I return from Baekke to find commoners complaining of slain guardian spirits, and a priest sat at my table. A *priest*!' She fairly spat the word out.

'And so I turn to you, little skald, because it strikes me that the choice, the danger, that you have twice foretold, is now come upon us.'

Leif nodded. 'That's what we thought. The shepherd, the crowned man – both my visions hinted at the White Christ.'

'And priests,' Thyre said, 'are ever jealous of the rights of their god. I've seen it in my dealings with the Saxons. Our faith is like the World Tree itself: a broad embrace that welcomes all to its branches. Odin, Thor, Frey; spirits of tree and stone; fetches, elves and dwarfs –' here she smiled at Leif – 'all find room in the boughs of our belief.'

Then the queen frowned. 'But the Christ-men's faith is like a bright and righteous flame, and once we let it in, it will consume the tree, and all that shelter in it. The flame will not admit of any but itself.'

Leif was impressed. Maybe he could make a poem out of the image . . .

'So I am not ready to suppose,' Thyre cut across his thoughts, 'that Folkmar's arrival, and these reported killings, are unconnected. The priest will seek to stamp out all traces of the old ways.'

The queen turned to Leif. '*You'll* be done for, for a start. There's no room for pagan skalds in a Christian court. Those who refuse to convert will be killed, like these creatures are being killed already. The question is: how is he doing it?'

'There's a beast,' said Astrid, and explained what they had learnt from the troll.

'Yet we have no proof,' Thyre mused. 'Haralt and his party will support the priest; that much is clear. And as my son's guest, I cannot simply throw him out. It would weaken our whole family in the eyes of the kingdom. Which makes it tempting to take stronger measures . . . but then again, were he to be killed, others would follow. Folkmar won't be acting alone, Haralt's right about that, and King Otto would send others after him. No; this must be done fairly, to show the Saxons they have no place in our lands. Which means we must have proof, if my husband is to be convinced of Folkmar's real danger.'

'I thought,' said Astrid, 'that we could go on a hunt for the beast. It can't be far away.'

Thyre's eyes flashed like summer lightning. 'Need I remind you, child, that you are forbidden from leaving Jelling?'

'N-no, Mother,' said Astrid, looking at the ground.

A hush descended on the grove. Bees thrummed through the blossom on a hawthorn bush. Somewhere above, the sleek brown shape of a pine marten skittered, and an alder leaf, sticky with sap, drifted slowly down to catch in Astrid's hair.

When next she looked up, her mother's face had softened.

'I just want to see you safe,' said Thyre, very slowly, each word a stone let fall from her hand. 'My family. My people.

95

Don't forget that the eastern half of the kingdom is mine by right, not your father's. And I won't –' her voice was rising despite herself – 'I won't see the old ways deserted, my people compelled to worship a god they've never known, and my husband lose all hope of entering Valhalla in the afterlife, all because one meddling, poxy pig of a Saxon convinces Gorm that Christ makes a better master than Odin.'

At times like this, her mother reminded Astrid of a wild cat at bay. Terrifying. Dangerous. Beautiful.

'So here's what you do.' Thyre had herself under control again. 'I can trust you both, and you're not stupid.' She glanced doubtfully at her daughter, but let it stand. 'That sets you apart from most here at Jelling. I want you to follow Folkmar. Spy on him. If you've any magic, little skald, now's the time to use it. I need to know his plans, his link to this beast of yours . . .'

She took a deep breath. 'And I need to know just how far my son Haralt is getting himself mixed up in all this.'

They nodded.

'Not a word to anyone,' said the queen. And then she vanished, back between the branches of the linden tree.

They stared after her.

'That's my mother,' said Astrid. 'Amazing, isn't she?'

FIFTEEN

ᚠᛁᛏ

Astrid had worked out Folkmar's weakness, and it had not been hard: food. He would rip, with cracked and yellow teeth, into a side of spring lamb, or veal, or demolish a whole brood of duckling at one sitting. The juices would run down his bristling series of chins, and then he would leer, and burp, and talk and talk and talk.

'Christ, a weakling? The Christ who was driving the moneylenders from the temple? You want power – my God is destroying whole cities when he is feeling so inclined. You never heard of Sodom? Of Gomorrah? Of the ten plagues of Egypt? Of the Great Flood . . . ?' And he would tell them, relishing each gory detail like a gobbet of flesh, and Astrid's appetite, once boundless, shrivelled away to nothing.

Once, with great cunning, she asked if there were any Bible tales about dragons, but his answer – though there was definitely a beast in it – was so confusing, all about 'revelations' and sounding more like a vision of Ragnarok, that Astrid was left none the wiser.

She found she was welcome now at the high table, waved over by Haralt to sit between him and Folkmar, as the priest spoke to King Gorm of the benefits of the Christian faith. The only trouble was avoiding Knut. Her elder brother refused to join them, but sat at the lower benches, and was quick to call her over to him and Thorbjorn as they ate.

She had never felt so wanted in her life; it made the horror of mealtimes in the dark, crowding hall a whole lot easier to bear. This was worst when, as now, she had to sit next to Folkmar. They were hip to hip – or rather, her hip was disappearing into the folds of his side.

Sometimes, presumably by accident, Folkmar's hand ended up on her thigh, and she had to poke it with her knife. *Ugh*.

Gorm fumbled for his drinking horn, and took a long, slow draught. 'What I want to know is: would all my subjects *have* to convert as well? And follow *just* this Christ alone?'

'Oh yes,' smiled Folkmar. 'It would be a wicked king indeed who is not saving all his people's souls also. Pagans are not being tolerated.'

'Pagans?' piped up Astrid.

'Pagans,' explained Folkmar, 'are like the lost sheep. They is needing – ahem – bringing back to the fold.'

'*Black* sheep?' she asked.

Haralt shot her a warning glance.

This was the point, she knew, that got Leif and her mother really cross. Everyone, they said, had to be free to choose.

So she looked up at her father, expecting an angry reply. But Gorm was nodding, deep in thought.

'I've always said we need a better way to keep the jarls in hand,' he said.

Folkmar beamed, and sunk his face into a whole roast suckling pig. A little blood spattered onto Astrid's hand. She pretended to ignore it.

ᚦ

'. . . So of course I see it would be a disaster if Gorm turned his back on the old gods,' she said to Leif.

They were sprawled on sweet-smelling straw bales in the stable where she now slept. It was dark, cool, private. The change of room had been, all things considered, an improvement.

'But all the same,' she continued, 'this Christ himself doesn't sound so bad. The way Folkmar puts it, he seems to be a great warrior.'

She paused. 'Though there was this time he sent a plague of frogs. Frankly, I think he lost his touch a bit there.'

Leif shot her a strange look. 'War, wrath, sin. Yes – that's Folkmar's god all right. But back at Hedeby, I knew Christians. And there, they spoke of peace, and love, and how to live a humble life and help others.'

'Well, that doesn't sound too bad either,' she said, and looked at him. 'If rather on the boring side. You never told me you were friends with any Christ-folk.'

'My grandmother and they were on bad terms. But one – a

woman – talked to me a lot. Johanna Svensdottir, that was her name; she was the first to really hear my gift for words, and said that one day I'd go far. She was a good person, and nothing like this Folkmar . . . But it's him that's here, not her.'

Astrid was silent. She had not yet chosen which god to follow above all others.

Leif went on. 'And we're not finding out enough like this. His plans – the beast – and *why* he's come at all; you saw the way that he looked at the stones. We'll have to watch when he thinks we're not there.'

'How?'

'Could we not ask your friend Nisse to spy?'

'No,' said Astrid at once. Little Nisse had moved to the stables too, and they could hear him scrabbling around above their heads. Clearly the spirit couldn't stand being near Folkmar. Well, she could understand *that* all right.

'I won't offend him by asking him to do something he'd hate,' she whispered, to avoid Nisse hearing. 'Besides, I think it's sweet he's come out here with me instead of joining his friends above the great hall. I can't send him away when he's chosen to stay. You'll have to think of something else.'

'In that case, it's time I tried some magic.'

|

It had never worked before, the old shaman's trick his grandmother had tried to teach him. But then, Leif told himself, he had never sought to work it so close to the Yelling Stones. Everything was so much more powerful here.

He lay under a cloak, in his place on the earthen bench that ran the length of the hall. He closed his mind to the world – bustling thralls, droning flies, dusty light – and concentrated on dark, fear, hunger and the press of small spaces.

Leif found himself remembering the hovel he had shared for most of his life with his Finn grandmother. It smelt of age, and sweat, and wild garlic, and he had sat in a damp corner coughing smoke and cauldron fumes.

That was the world he had always tried to escape – first through his mind, and then at last, for good.

But right now, he had to send himself back there. To imagine himself small, lonely and scared, tucked into a sheltering corner. His nose twitched.

A cat padded past, tail brushing the cloak. And Leif – lost in the trance – quivered with fright.

'Your king, he is jeopardised – his enemies accumulate around him now, he has not the escape!'

'It may be as you say, bishop, for there are few here to defend him. Perhaps it is time to strike?'

A single spindle of light shone into Astrid's old chamber, where Folkmar and Haralt sat closeted together. In the corners, where dust spooled, a mouse pricked up its ears. Deft-stepped, it scurried to the safety of the bed, darting up its headboard, to overlook the pair.

'It is good advice you are giving me, Highness. If I move

now, he is surrounded on three sides and his doom is near!'

Raised on its haunches, the mouse peered through the gloom. The vast priest and the tall prince were hunched about a table, poring over . . .

A game of hnefatafl! Leif – that is, the mouse – groaned with disappointment. Maybe there was no plot after all?

Then he ducked, as a walrus-ivory piece half his size came flying past his head. Haralt had brought his fist down on the playing board, scattering the pieces.

'Priest, I tire of this game, of all this talk of kingship! Nothing you have said changes the fact that Knut stands to inherit the throne, not me. And what price then your Christian Kingdom of Denmark?'

'But, sire, Our Lord tells us that patience is a virtue.'

'Patience! Is that why you spend half your nights sat outside, just staring at those old stones? To be virtuous?'

'Prince, you are mocking me. You know the strength of the Yelling Stones as well as any.'

'Old skalds' tales!' said Haralt. 'My father rules this land through a clever marriage and force of arms, not because of some magic rocks.'

'So, you do not believe Jelling is a place of power?'

'Of course it is.' Haralt almost spat. 'It lies on the Ox Road, halfway along the length of the realm. It's close enough to Vejle Fjord to reach the sea and islands quickly, but not so close to need defending from raiders. For a strong ruler, it's perfect. Now, if only you were to drain the marshes . . .'

Folkmar waved a fat hand dismissively. 'No, no. You tease me still. I mean *real* power, the power that is coming

102

from untold centuries of belief and worship.'

'Come now, bishop. Surely, this sort of superstition is the first thing to be stamped out, if we get our way and convert the kingdom?'

'Stamped out? Oh yes, just as you say!' Folkmar's piggy eyes were shining. 'But idols must be being crushed –' he squeezed his fist – '*because* they are powerful. Nothing is to challenge Our Lord's supremacy.'

'That's all very well,' said Haralt. 'But what about challenging my accursed *brother's* supremacy, eh? The man's a mountain, and what's more, his men are the best, most loyal fighters this side of Miklagard.'

'Certainly, Knut holds Jelling in his fist as a bear cradles an apple. But what if he were to depart from here?'

'Bah! Knut won't go a-viking, not with Father near his deathbed. He'll want to be here at the end.'

'But what I am saying is, were we to make it impossible for him to stay . . .'

Haralt grinned then, the blue dye in his teeth slashing his smile open horribly. He leant close to Folkmar, brow furrowed, and the mouse leant nearer too, and –

'Leif! Leif!' And Astrid was tugging at him where he lay on the bench, and he left the mouse, and the plotters in the dark, and never had his own body felt so heavy and hard. He tried to rise, to force his eyelids fully open, but he was too slow. And dimly he saw that as she turned from him Astrid was crying, the hot tears crumpling her beautiful face.

SIXTEEN

ᛋ

Why wouldn't Leif wake up? Astrid tugged at his tunic. She *needed* him.

Haralt was striding out of her old room, shouting at her to be quiet. She lost her head and ran in past him, slamming the door and flinging herself down on what used to be her bed. Ragged sobs escaped her as she heaved, and trembled, and seethed.

She bit her arm. Time passed. Slowly, she realised she wasn't alone.

'You know, princess, that is my bed now . . .' Astrid sat up, startled. For the first time she could make out Folkmar, sitting across from her in a massive chair.

His scent was everywhere – heavy, sweet, not half so repellent as she had expected. He must wear musk, or oils, like Muslims were said to.

Folkmar chuckled. 'I must say though, the bed fits you better! Me, my feet stick out, and my arms flop – thus.' He lolled hugely in his chair, looking so truly ridiculous that she couldn't help but giggle.

He scraped the chair closer. 'That is more like it,' he said. 'You should not be crying, when God gives you such a face.'

Astrid paused. Her heart was still racing, but now, more in anger than terror. She needed a way to fight back, but more than that, she needed to know her own mind: to be more than a piece in other people's games. In *men's* games.

'Folkmar,' she said. 'What does your Christ have to say about women?'

The huge man pursed his lips, scratched his pate.

'Well,' he said, 'is quite a lot. You know two of his most important followers were being women, for beginnings.'

'Just tell me one thing: can women marry for themselves? Here, a married woman may leave her man and keep her own wealth, but first we're bargained for, like – like cattle.' Her voice was bitter with emotion.

Folkmar rose, breathing hard with the effort. His glistening face grew animated. 'Now, Astrid, you are talking of a question being very near to my heart: marriage.'

He reached out with a trembling hand towards her face. 'Is anyone ever telling you, how beautiful you are being?'

'Oh, by Njord's fair feet, what is it with you men?!' Astrid sprang up fast as a falcon, and ran from the room.

ᚱ

Leif found her in the herb garden, walled from the wind. Astrid lay among rows of rosemary, picking at the scurvy grass that grew in clumps along the rocky border. She was face down, nose buried in the turf.

'Astrid?'

'Oh, it's you,' she spoke into the soil. 'Enjoyed your nap?'

'I wasn't asleep!' he protested, stung. 'I was being a mouse.'

At that, she looked up. Grass and mud clung to her red, wet face. 'A *mouse*?'

'I went into a trance to spy on your brother and Folkmar. They *do* have a plan. But you turned up before I found it out. Which reminds me. Why have you been crying?'

'I wasn't crying!'

He waited.

'All right, I was. Leif, look at me a moment. What do you see?'

'Mostly, dirt. And rage. And – a trick question?'

She sighed. 'Well, at least you admit that I've got a mind of my own.'

'Please, Astrid, tell me why you're so upset.'

She gestured at a patch of ground beside her. He sat. She gave him a leaf of scurvy-grass. He nibbled it.

'It's very peppery,' he offered.

She almost smiled. 'This morning, Knut sent for me,' she began. 'He wanted me to take a message . . .'

⁜

That morning, Astrid had been put at work in the yard, preparing overwintered leeks for a stew.

Thunder-faced, Knut appeared, and shouted to his sister. 'Astrid, take Hestur and ride over to Hellir. I've a message for Thorbjorn.'

'To Hellir? But I'm not allowed . . .'

He waved her objections aside. 'Tell Thorbjorn not to bring the men up to Jelling today. They're to stay put, and I'll join them for dinner. If he asks my reasons, tell him this: that the early summer heat prickles many men's nerves, and Hellir is cooler than Jelling when tempers run hot.'

Astrid nodded – a ride was more fun than cooking – and made to leave.

'Oh, and, Astrid,' he called after her. 'If Thorbjorn asks for anything else – anything, mind – be sure to let him have it.'

It was all very strange, but she saddled up eagerly enough. Knut must be trying to avoid a fight breaking out between his men and Haralt's. As for his last words – well, who cared? It was sunny and she was free. She might as well enjoy the moment.

Hellir lay just east of Jelling, and was where Knut's berserks lived when not at Gorm's hall. Astrid had hardly ever been there, though it was so close. The place was out of bounds to all women and children . . . and in any case, she remembered, gasping, you smelt Hellir before you saw it. Hestur bridled as the stench of sweat, blood and worse things flooded their nostrils.

Alighting a safe distance from the camp, Astrid tethered Hestur to a branch. She knew too well the fate of horses left unattended within Hellir. Mustering her courage, she strode down the single dusty street. 'Thorbjorn!' she yelled.

The place seemed deserted. On either side ran squalid huts, roofed with turf, more like forest caves than proper houses. Not a door was open. Feeling very small, Astrid went up to one and knocked.

No reply.

She tried the handle; it didn't budge. It felt as if a heavy object was wedged against the door from inside.

Now she thought about it, the whole place had the air of a camp under siege. And it was nearly noon – even warriors couldn't be sleeping in *this* late . . .

A wheelbarrow, overturned, split apart. A battleaxe abandoned in the dust.

Smoke rising from a burnt-out hut, a pine tree toppled to lie in solitary ruin amid the embers, like a spear resting in the ribcage of the roof.

Just *what* had been going on here?

Too late, Astrid had the answer. And she began to run, to run for her life, as a shadow fell across the path, and behind her, she heard the beat of heavy wings.

It was here; the beast was here, now, coming closer. A single door lay ahead of her at the street's end, and Astrid hurtled towards it, slamming her body against the cankered oak planks.

The planks held firm. The sound of wings grew louder. She could have wept.

'Open up!' she panted, breathless. 'Please!' She beat at the lock with her fist.

The wings were silent. In the sudden hush, Astrid dared to hope. Had it gone?

And then she heard the lazy tread of heavy feet, coming down the street towards her.

Think, she told herself. A lock: it must be Thorbjorn's door, the best hut in Hellir. It was the lock that kept her out, nothing more.

If Leif were here, he would talk to it, ask it to open. She couldn't do that. Could she?

Astrid opened her mouth, but found no words. The footsteps were nearer now.

No words – but a tune that rose unsought to her lips; that danced upon her tongue.

From behind her came a fierce heat, a harsh smell, a dryness. The beast was moments away.

And Astrid sang: a nervous, queer little melody – a rising scale with a quiver at the end. The sound of a secret almost told. She was searching for one final note to end the tune, to form the key . . .

And she had it! With a *click* and a *creak*, the lock turned, and the door swung.

A metallic rasping from behind her and a rushing of air, but she was through through *through*, and slamming the door behind her.

An inhuman shriek of fury from outside shook the hut. Frozen, Astrid listened, as the beast paced about, footfalls heavy in the dust. At last she heard the *whump* and *whirr*, as once more its wings churned the air, and then it faded, and faded, and the beast was gone.

She wouldn't cry. Not yet. She still had a message to deliver.

'Thorbjorn?' she said.

The darkness in the hut was near total. It stank worse than outside, but there was a new note in the stench – honey, sickly sweet. Astrid peered into the black.

The smell came from young mushrooms, growing through the floor, bulbous pale heads thrusting up from fat white stems. She bent closer. Death caps, she decided, and shrunk away from the fleshy growths.

'Who's there?' The growl came from the depths of the hut.

'It's me. Astrid.' She crept further in. Something hard cracked under her foot. Bone? It flashed whitely as it rolled aside, into the gloom. She bit her lip.

'Stay back,' said the voice, thick and brown. 'It isn't safe.'

'I know,' she stammered. 'The beast was right here! But it's gone now. And I've . . . I've got a message for you, from Knut. Where are you?'

The smell now hung so thick it might have been grease in the air. Roof and walls were low and close, hemming her in, but she'd come this far. And squinting ahead, she thought she saw a figure, covered in furs.

Somewhere, flies were droning.

The figure turned its face to hers – except, it *couldn't* be a face. It was too long, too heavy, too low down.

The thing – Thorbjorn? – growled again, enormously loud. Not a man's growl, but a bear's.

A huge, furred limb reached out for her. She saw teeth, and she ran, ran, ran.

Everything she'd heard about berserkers had been true. She was out in the sun and racing to Hestur, and everywhere were bears, bears in doorways, bears in the street, but she was in the saddle and kicking away and Hellir was behind her, behind her.

ᛒ

'And that's why the beserkers were all in hiding. Men turning into bears – that's just the sort of pagan magic Folkmar wants to stamp out. If the beast is following his orders, then no wonder it attacked Hellir,' said Astrid.

'It must have taken you for one of them. It's a shame that you never *saw* the beast.'

'You'd never have dared look either. Besides, there was no time.' She glared. 'So anyway, I came straight to you, and you were asleep, so I went to my bed. Folkmar was there –'

'In your bed?'

'In a chair. I was so mad at Knut for sending me that I asked all about Christ, and –'

'Astrid, not you too? What were you thinking?'

'You needn't worry about that. Turns out Folkmar's less interested in my "soul" than in . . . well . . . I swear, Haralt and Knut, they're as bad as each other.'

'I don't understand . . . '

'They've *both* been looking to get me married off to suit themselves. I see it now . . . parading me before their favourites like a prize mare. Thorbjorn or Folkmar: which is worse?'

'Folkmar would never marry a pagan.'

'But what if they win, Leif? *What if they win*, and we're all made Christians? Or what if they lose, and I'm given to Thorbjorn instead?'

111

She was tearing up whole clumps of herbs, her arms shaking.

Leif went to her. 'They use you. All of them. It's what they do. Your brothers, Thyre – all they want is power.'

He was getting angry too. 'These tall, pale lords, with blood upon their hands – they only care for keeping this land theirs.'

Astrid glared, but Leif didn't notice. 'And where are you and me in all of this? Just pieces on a board, moved on a whim.' He remembered the ivory gaming piece, sent flying by Haralt's fist.

'That's my family you're talking about, Leif.' Her words were slow, hard, measured.

'I know – and do they act like it to you?'

'I don't care. You've no right to go casting slurs on those you've come to serve.'

'Astrid, what is this –'

Furious, she cut across him. 'No one's going to sell me to another man against my will. But you, you've sold yourself already, to my father. Remember? You're sworn to follow him; you eat at his bench. So don't go biting the hand that feeds you, all right? What've you got against them anyway? The king's not hurt you.'

'In Iceland,' Leif shot back, 'they have no king. Just poets, traders, farmers – and it seems to work all right!'

'Well why don't you just GO to Iceland then!'

He had no answer.

'I'll tell you why –' she was shouting now – 'because you *love* all this. The power. The importance. The courtliness. You say you don't but you love it, because it makes you think this is where things happen, and it makes you feel like you're a part of it all. You're scared of Christians because they've no need of skalds – what's the point of someone who can make up poems about gods no one believes in anyway – and you're not going to leave Jelling, because so long as you *are* the king's skald, you can say you matter!'

She wiped some grass-green spit from her mouth. 'Besides, you'd never leave these silly stones until you've *proved* yourself somehow, which is, by the way, just like a boy and *incredibly* boring. And now you're all agog with this big danger, and your sacred destiny – you get to make the choices, you're going to save the trolls – and you know what, Leif? You know what? *Good* for you, but leave me out of it, because I *do* know what I want, and if anyone's running off to Iceland, it's me. So don't pretend we're in this together, because they may be *my* family, and your skin may be darker than ours, but you're more one of them than I'll ever be, and I've had *enough*!'

She stared at him, face flushed, daring him to bite back. There was a hush. Bees flitted round the rosemary.

'You wouldn't, though, would you?' said Leif, at last. 'Leave, I mean?'

'No,' she admitted. 'Not now everything's started to happen. Not until it's over, one way or the other. I just wish . . .'

'Yes?'

'All this magic – I just wish it didn't have to be so *destructive*. Bears, beasts, storms, fire – why can't anything just be *fun*?'

Leif rose. 'You know, that sounds like a challenge.'

SEVENTEEN

ᛋᛁᚾᛏ�miᚾ

'Bleagh! This mead might as well be pond water . . .'

'You should've brought some herbs from the garden.'

'I did,' said Astrid, suddenly remembering. She brought forth a clump of jagged leaves with young yellow flowers. 'No idea what they are,' she said, nibbling one, 'but they taste interesting enough.' She shredded the plant into the bucket of honeyed liquid.

They had broken into a storehouse, split the first cask they'd found, and filled a pail. Now, they were taking turns to raise the pitcher to their lips.

''S the same,' she shrugged, mead dripping from her nose as she raised her head. She was disappointed. 'You promised to show me something *amazing*. You do know this is *this* year's mead, right? There's no yeast in it yet – it's just honey and water. You can't even get tipsy on the stuff.'

'Oh, Astrid. We're not trying to get *drunk*.'

'Oh. Then what are we doing?'

'I know a way,' said Leif, tapping his nose, 'to make it taste like Kvasir's brew itself.'

'More spells? Is that the "fun" you promised me?'

'When I am done, this mead will free us from ourselves: for just one night, we can forget. Leave ourselves behind, if you like. I hope . . .'

'You *hope*?'

'I've never tried it! But it can't be hard – all that you need are three runes, and a rhyme.' Leif hunched over the pail. Astrid leant closer, interested in spite of herself.

With his forefinger, Leif traced a shape in the liquid: ᚠ.

'Wealth will undo kins'-ease;
Wolves too live among trees.'

'Fe,' he said. 'That's for wealth.' They watched as the rune faded.

He bent again. ᛚ, he drew.

'Water falls from on high;
Fine gold things please the eye.'

'Log. That's for waterfall.' Again the letter vanished.

'Last one,' he said, etching the final shape: ᚱ.

'Riding ruins the horse;
Reginn forged the best sword.'

'Reid, for riding.'

As he spoke, the drink rippled like a lake in a storm, and bubbles bucked and sprayed as breakers on a wave. Astrid goggled, and the froth cleared, leaving a liquid no longer pale yellow, but rich red gold.

'Wealth, waterfall, riding,' she muttered. 'Well, either a troupe of tiny golden horses is about to dive down my throat, or this is going to taste incredible.'

'Those both sound pretty good,' said Leif, and drank.

ᛦ

It was midnight when they staggered from the hut, their quarrel quite forgotten. Whatever Leif's magic was, it had certainly worked.

'They're all asleep!' said Astrid. 'Jelling is ours!' She ran into the hall, arms wide and flapping, '*kak kak kak*'-ing as she went.

Leif tripped after her.

She was standing on the high table and spinning on the spot, her dress flowering round her waist, a blur of close-cut breeches below.

He stumbled down the hall, tottering into the earth bench along the left-hand side. The only sleepers lay across from him – Haralt's men – and their snoring rose to the rafters. They had feasted well, and drunk better – the snores said as much – but Leif was still wary.

'Where's the rest of them?' he hissed.

'Hiding in Hellir. And good riddance! They're un*bear*able.' She collapsed into fits of giggling.

'Shh,' he said. 'These ones will wake . . .'

He tried to vault up onto the dais, missed, and fell back heavily on a pile of abandoned cloaks.

Astrid sniggered. 'Leif sore-arse.'

He put out his hand on something hairy, and held up a felt mask. Then another: wolfsheads. 'Oo! We had these at Hedeby,' he said.

He tossed one at Astrid. She lunged, missed, overbalanced and toppled to the floor in a heap. It was Leif's turn to snigger as she struggled up, shrugging out of her rucked-up dress, a pale blue pool of wool beneath her feet.

'I could be a boy,' she said, looking down at her tunic and riding breeches.

'Not with Sif's gold hanging to your shoulders.'

Roughly, she grabbed her hair in one hand, piling it atop her head. With the other, she jammed the mask on over it. 'Now?' she asked, from somewhere beneath the long grey muzzle.

He shook his head, laughed, donned his own mask. '*Rrreuf!*'

She whined back at him in imitation of wolves they had known. Then, 'Come on,' she said, 'I've had an idea.'

Taking her hand, Leif allowed himself to be led – in a less than straight line – to the door on the left, behind the throne.

She turned to him. 'Knut's got some wolf pelts from the hunt! And he's gone down to Hellir to help protect his men . . .'

She tried the door. ''S locked!' Remembering, she opened her mouth to sing the lock open. Just in time, Leif clapped a hand across her mouth. 'Too loud,' he hissed.

She glared at him, deflated.

Leif tugged the hem of his sleeve, pulling off a few frayed fibres. These he sucked, and thrust into the iron lock. 'Yarn-jarn, spittle-lykill,' he slurred. The door clicked open.

'Howdo do that?'

'I've *no* idea!'

They edged into the room. Draped across an empty bed, clear in the light of a low-burning oil lamp, were two shaggy wolf skins. Astrid grabbed them. Then she yelped.

Haralt was sitting in the other bed, facing right at her.

⋮

'Oops, forgot you,' she said. Haralt didn't move. Spread open on his lap was an odd thing – thin scribbled sheaves between large leather boards. Now she looked more closely, his eyes were closed and he was clearly sound asleep.

'Wassat?' she whispered, pointing.

'A book,' breathed Leif, tiptoeing over. His hands itched to pick it up, to possess it. He squinted at the Latin words. Haralt had underlined a section.

> . . . *concerning the third stage of conversion. In discussing the treatment of false idols, St Gregory states that, when gentler methods fail, the sacred places and totems of such peoples must be deliberately destroyed, thus demonstrating the powerlessness of their gods. In just such a manner did Moses cast the golden calf into the flame . . .*

'What does it say?' said Astrid.

Leif looked at the spidery foreign symbols. 'I have absolutely no idea.' He frowned at the book. 'But he hasn't got very far . . .'

ᚦ

The tread of heavy feet startled them both: someone was coming.

'C'mon,' hissed Astrid, and shoved him out into the hall; kept shoving till they were out under the stars.

'Let's put the skins on!' She had already thrown one pelt around her shoulders. Now she flung back her head, and howled.

'Shh,' said Leif, again. 'Not here!' And now *he* shoved, and she shoved back, and they were both rolling on the grass.

The Yelling Stones thrummed in the quiet of the night. *Throb* and *thud*, *throb* and *thud*, as regular and vital as a heart's beat in their pricked-up ears. They scurried and scampered on all fours, yipping and yelping past the mound.

'Leif,' said Astrid – or tried to. All that came out was a bark. Something very strange was happening as they raced past the stones; something that rippled the cool night air and ran right through their bodies.

And then – then she forgot. Forgot everything. She was ahead of Leif as they left the hall behind, and she glanced over her shoulder with a grin as she dropped down to the earth. Peddling her hind legs, she stuck up her tail and waggled it at the moon. He growled, leapt, and over they rolled again.

119

She came up on top, astride his belly, and their muzzles clashed in the greying night.

'Catch me,' he heard – though not exactly in words – and the chase was on.

The night was a tapestry of scent and sound, streaked and shot through all around with trails and traces that perfumed and trickled, cobwebbing odours of coming and going. And through this thicket of reeking and rustling, the two figures ran, and romped, and melded into night. Howls serrated the silence, falling and rising in eager harmony.

॥

Blood was hot; hunger was cold. This much she knew. Everything was streaks of grey, blurred beneath a pale-faced moon. But the *smells* – they were thick bright ropes of warm, furry taste, pulling her this way, pulling her that.

Not this one though – this smell meant danger. The boy-wolf nipped her flank and she spun, growled, stared him into silence.

Something was coming.

A man, ambling through the trees. He swung at flowers and ferns with the long, straight iron-stick that stretched from his paw. Sound was coming from his mouth – something between the lowing of a cow and the mewl of a tomcat.

The other wolf crouched, hackles low, and she shouldered him back. *Wait.*

Two other men followed the first. They were stalking it,

she realised, trying not to be seen. One was tall and thin, the other enormously fat.

You could feed a pack on that one for a whole winter, she thought.

Tall nodded to Fat, and Fat let out a series of low noises, passing his paw across his chest before pointing at the first man, still strolling on ahead of them. Tall spat, turned, and strode back into the dark.

Then the night air throbbed with the beat of wings. A bright light descended – too bright to look at – and she flung herself, flat and panting, down in the tall grasses.

She smelt strange things for which she had no name – sand, spices, searing heat – and heard a cry, a whirring, a thud.

Then there was the fire-smell in her nostrils. She whimpered, afraid, and cracked an eyelid open.

The first man lay still, reeking of death – she licked her lips – and Fat was speaking again, pointing further ahead of him. The bright, winged shape lifted into the air, and sped away eastwards, trailing flame. Fat bent, touching his paw to the dead one, before shambling off in the direction Tall had taken.

The two wolves crept closer to the body, snuffling and squinting. She cocked her head on one side, trying to work something out.

Dead man's shape was all wrong.

EIGHTEEN

The horns blasted redly through the forest, borne in on the light of the morning, flooding trees and ferns in sunshine and discord. The clamour swam around two sleepers, cradled in the roots of a giant beech. From beneath their torn and matted pelts they stirred, and rose, and yawned.

'Ungh . . .' said Leif. And then: 'My head!'

'Not so loud,' moaned Astrid, pointlessly. The horns had not stopped.

'What's that noise?' he asked.

'Summons . . . ugh . . . my tongue's like a sand spit.'

'My tongue's like old birch bark. And my head feels like Thor's anvil. What summons?'

'It's calling everyone to Jelling. On pain of death.'

'That's nice,' said Leif, and settled back down under the furs.

'That means us, too.'

'Oh.'

Astrid stood. Then wished she hadn't. Then, so that at

least she had someone to share the pain, she heaved Leif to his feet. 'We'd best leave the skins,' she said. 'Look at the state of them. Leif . . .'

'Yes?'

'I think we saw the beast.'

'Did we? Yes – and Folkmar. And a body . . .'

'And – and Haralt? I can't remember it properly.'

'Nor can I. And Leif?'

'Yes?'

'Did we become . . . I mean, *were* we . . . ?'

'I think so.'

'Wow.'

'Wow.'

The hall was nearly full when they arrived. Leif and Astrid crammed into his space on the bench. Folkmar had Haralt's seat at the high table; Haralt himself had the floor. Both of them looked very tired . . . and very smug.

Hands on hips, Haralt paced about, waiting till all the places were filled. Then he turned to address his father. 'King Gorm, I appeal to you to resolve a dispute that has arisen between me and a person or persons unknown.' He spoke dry and fast, like a shower of pebbles.

Gorm shifted in his seat. 'Could you not have called upon Knut, your brother? He is Gothi of all this company.'

'No, Father, for Knut is caught up in the case I bring before you.' Gorm glowered.

'What is the nature of this dispute, my son?'

'It concerns the killing of one of my bondsmen, Harmsorgi the Converted.'

The room rippled with surprise.

'When was the killing?' said Gorm.

'Late last night, in the forest between here and Hellir.'

Astrid caught Leif's eye. 'The body,' she said. 'I remember . . .'

'Hush,' said Weland, at her left.

Knut's gruff voice rang out. 'If this is a killing case, it should be held over till the Thing at Ringsted, and come before our uncle Thorlagi, the law-speaker.'

A murmur of assent met his words, though both Gorm and Haralt glared at him.

Thyre's cold voice chimed in. 'You forget yourself, my son. The Thing itself agreed years ago that the king at Jelling holds the right to act as law-speaker when the Thing is not in session.'

Several voices rose at this, all arguing at once.

'What are they talking about?' hissed Leif.

'The Thing,' Astrid murmured, 'is the great law-meeting of all the free Danes. Every year they gather at Ringsted to settle their arguments. Father's always wanted to hold it here, with him – or Knut, now – as judge.'

Leif frowned. 'In Iceland –'

She kicked him just in time. 'Oh, shut up about Iceland. It works like this. If the two parties can't agree, they have a choice. They fight, either with weapons or with words –'

'A flyting,' put in Leif. 'I've heard of them. A fight with words is known as a flyting.'

'Of course, you would know about that,' she whispered. 'Anyway, the loser – if he lives – has to pay the wergild: the blood-price.'

'And the outcome of the "fight" is binding?'

'Oh yes. It's all done under oath. But there won't be a fight here – my brothers may be idiots, but even they aren't that stupid. It would destroy our family. They'll settle it somehow or other.'

Leif went very quiet. A contest, one on one, to settle a question . . . yes, that could do the trick . . .

'It is decided, then,' said Gorm at last. 'I shall judge between you in this affair.'

He tugged an iron ring from his finger, and threw it upon the table.

'Now,' he mused, 'we need the blood of a third party to honour this oath-ring . . .'

All heads on the dais turned to Folkmar, who blanched white.

Thyre took Folkmar's thick wrist in her left hand, her knife in her right, and scored a narrow line across his palm. He grunted, and the sweat beaded on his brow, but he bore it well enough.

Thyre pressed the ring to the cut, and returned it to the table. Both Knut and Haralt swore their oaths over it, Knut at a bellow, Haralt in a drawl.

'I call on my cousin Grey-cloak, to swear and to bear witness,' said Haralt.

The man came forward, and made his oath. 'Last night, disturbed by noises in the dark, my companion Harmsorgi would not lie down to sleep with us, his fellows, but declared he would take a stroll down to Hellir.'

Many backs in the hall stiffened at this.

Grey-cloak went on. 'We counselled him against it, but the ale in his blood spoke the louder, I think. Taking with him his sword, but no other friend, he broke from the hall, and those of us who made to follow could not find him in the dark.'

'Did he say anything further to his purpose?' asked Gorm.

'He said he fancied he would hunt a bear this night, and that with Christ to light his path, he didn't think there would be too much trouble from thunder and lightning.'

The hall erupted. Men were on their feet everywhere, fists clenched.

'It's a good thing no weapons are allowed during trials,' said Astrid.

Leif nodded. The berserkers near him were hurling insults at Haralt's men across the hall, whose leader – and his royal cousin – stood, still and silent, at the centre of the word-storm.

'Silence!' Gorm hammered weakly on the table. Gradually, the noise died down.

'Where was he found, and in what state?' said Gorm.

'In the woods, a bowshot from Hellir,' said Haralt. 'His friends found him at first light, his corpse already cold.'

Images were flooding back to Astrid. Grey trees – a bright shape – a body . . .

Thyre stood up, ashen-faced. She looked from one son to another, her pain clear for all to see. 'There were wolves in the forest last night,' she said. 'We heard the howls.'

'No wolf caused his wounds,' said Haralt.

Thyre tried again. 'The thralls found henbane missing from the garden. Perhaps this unlucky man poisoned himself with the herbs?'

'Lady,' said Grey-cloak, 'his wounds came from no plant.'

'Then perhaps, a fall?' she offered in desperation.

'Mother,' cut in Haralt, 'Harmsorgi was found without his head.'

|

'Knut,' said Gorm, when the fuss had died down, 'have you, or any of your men, on oath, knowledge of these events?'

'No, on my honour,' said Knut. 'But one of them, Karl Bersi, has not answered the summons, and none has seen him since last night.'

'Then, brother,' said Haralt, 'I demand the blood-price from you, as his liege, and your word that no such thing will happen again. We cannot risk further bloodshed on the part of your men, and you obviously can't control them.'

'It's not true,' hissed Astrid. 'It wasn't this Karl Bersi, it was the beast. We *saw* it!'

'I know,' said Leif, 'but try telling *them* that. And then, try explaining *how* we saw it . . .'

She closed her mouth, stumped. No one would believe them.

Knut strode forward, leaping lightly from the dais. He loomed over his brother, broad and brown. He raised his mighty arm – only to lay it on Haralt's shoulder.

'Since first I heard this news, little brother, I have been thinking of what is right. You shall have your blood-price when next we meet, but it shall be in Irish gold.'

'But he'll know it was the beast too,' whispered Astrid, on the verge of tears. 'Why doesn't he *say* so?'

'He would have to accuse his brother's guest,' said Leif. 'Knut's none too sharp, but he won't start a feud. He'll take his men away to protect them, but to protect your family as well.'

Knut turned, his words taking in the whole hall. 'Truly, it is no good thing that grown warriors stay at home and swelter in the summer sun. I am taking twelve ships, and going a-viking. If it is Thor's will that I return, and that we meet again –' and now, he was looking straight at his father – 'it shall be with the crown of Dublin to add to our titles.'

And he swept from the hall, all his men streaming in his wake; a surging mass of men, as if already Knut had put to sea.

Astrid, her face stricken, stared after him. He never turned, never gave her so much as a glance. And what if she never saw him again?

Leif meanwhile looked back to the dais, in time to see a smile flicker between Folkmar and Prince Haralt.

NINETEEN

ᚼᛏᚼᛁ

'So what do we do now?' Leif asked Astrid.

'You're the one who's destined to make the choices, remember? The one who the stones want to stop Folkmar – the one who gets trolls all excited.' She was being unfair, and she knew it, but Knut's departure was an open wound in her chest, and she was in no mood to be kind.

'I know. And as fate's champion . . . I'm asking you.'

She smiled, just a little. 'I say we track down the beast. There must be a way to kill it, or send it away, or something . . .'

Leif grinned. 'I thought you'd say that. So: tonight?'

'If Mother's back.' Thyre had gone to Ribe to see Knut off. Astrid blushed. 'I . . . I want her blessing.'

'You're scared?'

She nodded.

'Me too. But we can't let it keep killing. There is one snag, though.'

'What?'

'How do we find it?'

Astrid thought for a bit. 'Can you *really* talk to things? To trees . . . and animals?'

'Yes.'

'Then ask Valvigs.'

⋮

The glorious white bird mewled its discontent. Nothing Astrid did would convince him to fly.

'He's never been like this before,' she said. 'It's as if he's afraid.'

'It seems as if the sky's no longer safe.' Leif bent to the falcon. 'Valvigs, falcon of slaughter . . .'

The bird swivelled round its hunkered head, giving him the full force of its eyes.

Leif bent to the gyrfalcon and whispered in its ear. Valvigs cawed once, spread his beautiful wings, and rose into the air. Leaning back, they saw him circling, wider and wider, his white form black against the sun. His spiral took him north . . . west . . . south . . . east . . . and on east, lower, over the river gorge – and now he was plummeting down, swooping, wings tucked, racing back to them.

Astrid smoothed his ruffling feathers, petting the panicked bird. 'We've got our answer then,' she said. 'The Grejsdal Valley. There are caves there.' She shivered, remembering her encounter with the fiery, massive beast. 'Perfect for a dragon.'

'Look, if it's a dragon, I'll eat my hat.'

'You haven't got a hat.'

'Then I'll eat *your* hat.'

She thought about this. 'The beaver-fur, or the marten?'

'I think we're straying from the point somewhat . . .'

'I've got an old felt one somewhere. You could eat that, I suppose.'

A clatter of hoofs drowned out Leif's reply.

:

Thyre swept through Jelling like a tempest.

'The queen's back from Ribe,' said Leif. 'Come on!'

Until she saw her mother stride alone into the hall, Astrid had not really believed that Knut could have gone for good. Surely, it had all been just an act – a dramatic gesture to impress Haralt – he couldn't really have sailed away, leaving her behind. But now the queen was back, alone, and her brother was setting a course for the west.

For a moment, she imagined it was the salt spray of seawater on her face, and that she too had just taken ship from Ribe, that bustling harbour of spices, silks and foreign faces. Then she wiped away the tears, and she and Leif hurried after Thyre, caught up in her wake.

'My lady, we have news about the beast,' said Leif, snatching at the queen's flowing blue robe, just inside the hall doors.

'Beast or priest?' said Thyre. Her face was grim-set, full of purpose – she was clearly only half listening to him.

'Both!' said Astrid. She darted her head about – good – no one was in earshot. 'We saw what killed Harmsorgi. Sort of . . .'

'Sort of?' said Thyre.

'Our eyes were dazzled by the creature's light,' put in Leif. 'But we were in the woods that night, and saw Folkmar follow, and point, and then the beast flew down and lopped off poor Harmsorgi's head!'

'And then,' added Astrid, 'the priest pointed towards Hellir, and the beast hurried away. We think it must have killed Karl Bersi too, and disposed of the body somehow. Maybe it ate him.'

'Can you swear to this?' asked Thyre, in a low tone.

Leif shook his head. 'To you, maybe, but not before the court.'

'Why not?

'Because,' said Astrid, eyes on the ground, 'because we saw another man with Folkmar in the woods. It was Har—'

'Do not say it!' said the queen. Her face had paled. 'I will not have it said, though I suspected as much from the first. I see now why there can be no oath-taking on this matter.' Now it was Thyre's turn to glance around, uncertain. It was the first time Leif had seen her looking less than the ruler of all she surveyed.

'Haralt has stolen a march on us. Knut had to take his men abroad to stave off a bloodbath, that's clear enough. Yet I wish he'd left *someone* behind. Weland, Thorbjorn – they're all gone, and the only warriors here are Haralt's men.'

She laughed – a laugh that rang hollow in that huge space. 'Two women and a boy to save a king, and a kingdom. I'll do my best to stop my husband taking the Cross. But I can do nothing against Folkmar's beast – nothing to protect my people, and the weird folk they believe in.'

'About that,' said Astrid. 'We've decided. Leif and me. We're going hunting.'

The queen's eyes flashed. Her nostrils flared.

'Leif has magic,' Astrid went on. 'And I could track it – we know roughly where it is. There's no one else. We'll be careful.'

Thyre bit her lip. For a long moment, her face was a mass of fighting thoughts and fears.

'Let no one see you,' she said at last. 'And wait until dark. I have something planned for tonight's dinner, and it may give you protection against this strange, winged fury. And, Astrid,' she said, eyes moistening.

'Yes?'

'Know that I love you.'

†

Neither Astrid nor Leif had much of an appetite that evening. Astrid had been forced once more to sit alongside Folkmar, who was leering at her hungrily. She shifted in discomfort. At least, this close to the priest, she was safe from whatever was out there, in the darkness, in the gorge. But did not Folkmar himself present a second sort of danger, almost equally horrible? All things considered, she'd rather take her chances with a dragon . . .

After the pitiful meal, Thyre rose to speak. 'Knut, our beloved heir, has now gone west, to add new lustre to our kingdom's crown. But, ever the gift-giver, he sent back several arm-rings of silver, to remember him in his absence.'

133

Those who remained on the benches stirred, their interest quickened. Thyre dumped a clinking sack upon the table.

'Those rings were too few to bestow upon all the loyal liegemen in this hall. So before I returned from Ribe, I visited the silversmith, and had him recast the metal, so that all might share this bounty.'

From the sack, she drew forth tangled handfuls of shining pendants, each set upon a leather thong. 'It is my wish that each person in this hall who honours Gorm as king, and Knut his son, should receive the mark of it in silver, to bear proudly upon their chests. Let every man, woman and child come up and take their due!'

There was a rush to the table. Leif marvelled at the queen's cunning. To work on greed, and pride, and shame at once! But his admiration was redoubled as he reached the table, and saw the pendants close up.

Folkmar was peering forward with great interest at the pile of silver. Thyre turned to him with a broad smile. 'See, Saxon, with what skill our smiths work their metal! It is a new fashion in the towns, I hear, to bear one's beliefs for all to see – and look here: the smith has poured the silver into the shape of a hundred Thor's hammers!'

Even those of Haralt's men who had been baptised were seizing their portion of jewellery – to refuse a gift was unlucky, if not downright dangerous when presented in such terms. Astrid and Leif did likewise, hanging the tiny hammers – symbols of the thunder god – around their necks. Folkmar slumped back in his chair, a sickly smile wobbling his face.

TWENTY

ᛏᚹᛏᚢᚱᚾ

'I still say we should break into Weland's armoury in Hellir. It'll be deserted now, and I'd feel better with a sword,' said Astrid.

'You have your knife, and I my tongue,' said Leif. 'They're sharp enough, if things come to a fight. But if we're seen, I reckon we should run.'

They had made good progress – the moon was full – and it was easy enough to follow the wind of the river, between the walls of rock on either side. Now they were passing the place where first they'd met, and Leif had driven off the wolves. Underfoot, the scrabble of needles, roots and pine cones had given way to a springy bank; the whip of bristling spruces in their faces had thinned to the occasional trail of willow branches, raking through their hair like dead men's fingers.

Neither spoke, but Leif let his hand hang beside him and, in between the shadow and the silence, Astrid took it in her own.

'We must be close,' she whispered. Her right hand sought the hilt of her knife; now she had two things to hold on to.

Leif's free hand, with nothing to grip, had begun to shake. 'How can you tell?' he said.

'Last time we went out at night, you were jumping out of your skin at the least little noise.'

'Thanks for reminding me . . .'

'Well? It's been ages since we heard *anything*.'

It was true. Even the river on their right seemed to be holding its breath, its flat waters, oily in the night, creeping along with the stealth of a snake. They were walking on its high bank, between the water and the rock face, and every step of their leather-shod feet was a drum beat in their ears. *Thud. Thud. Thud.*

'*Squeak!*'

Leif leapt half out of his boots at the unexpected sound. 'What did you do *that* for?' he hissed, for it had been Astrid, squealing almost in his ear. She had a hand clapped over her mouth. With the other, she pointed.

Half in, half out of the water, a mark had been left in the mud. The size of a shield, sunk deep, with four smaller prints on the landward side. And beyond each of these, a long, cruel scratch: Astrid's knife would have fit in any one of them.

Leif edged left and up. Mutely, he gestured. Another print. And another. They led up out of the river, arcing round to follow its path downstream. They were huge. They were fresh. They were the footprints of a gigantic –

'I still say it's a dragon,' whispered Astrid. 'Leif, when we find this thing . . . do we have a plan?'

'I thought we'd hide until it falls asleep. And then, a spell . . . or, we could stab its heart . . . ?'

'What if it doesn't go to sleep?'

'I'm sure, if I can just find the right words . . .'

'What if you can't?'

'We'll be lucky. We always are. All right?'

It wasn't much comfort, thought Astrid, whose luck had never seemed especially good.

But I'm braver than him, she told herself. And so she had to go on.

ᚠ

They crept along, following the tracks, past scrub and gorse and overhanging rock. To their left, the cliffs were fissuring into caves – blackly gaping mouths from which anything might emerge – but the prints never led into any of them, and so they were forced to turn their shoulders to those awful holes, and keep their eyes before them.

'Astrid, I've been thinking,' Leif said at last.

'As if I wasn't scared enough already.'

'These tracks led up from out of the river . . .'

'And?'

'And the river flows out of Lake Faarup . . .'

'So, what are you trying to get at?'

'Last time we were out at night you told me the lake leads right down to the underworld. And anything could swim up out of it. Well . . . what if what we're tracking came from there . . . from the underworld?'

'Why would Folkmar's beast be coming from a pagan place? Unless *our* Hel is the same as the Christian Hell . . . But they sound so different. Theirs is hot, for one thing . . .'

'That wasn't what I was thinking,' he said. 'I meant, what if these tracks are not the beast's?'

Astrid didn't answer. She had stopped dead. The night was cold, yet she could feel sweat beading on her palms.

They had come to a widening of the gorge. The river arced round to the right, cutting a sheer channel through the crumbling rock wall on the near side, but leaving a wide bank of earth and scree on the inside of the loop. The bank shelved up gently, breaking into rocks and trees that stretched to meet the sky. A couple of straggling spruces clung to the cliff face, which rose, straight and bleak as bone, a jutting mass of rock awash in cool moonlight. High, high up, remote and unreachable, one cave pocked the wall of grey. And down at their feet, stone met water, and the mud bank vanished, and with it, all trace of the paw prints.

Wherever the beast was, it was not before them.

At a loss, the two of them, dwarfed in that harsh, sheer space – it might have been made for giants rather than men – stared at the rock wall. And, gradually, they noticed something else. The tracks had gone . . . And so had the silence.

From behind them, came the sound of heavy breathing.

↑

There was no wind that night, yet the hairs on the back of Leif's neck, which had begun to stand on end, were moved by a warm breath that came and went with the sound behind them. It almost tickled. And, with the breathing, came an overwhelming smell.

It smells like my grandmother, at the end, thought Leif.

And Astrid thought, *It is the smell of death*.

Their hearts were two caged blackbirds, beating at their bars. Beat one. Beat two. Beat three.

They turned together. Poised on a rocky outcrop, a spear's throw from where they stood, was . . . not a dragon. Not the bright winged beast. But a massive black hound.

Its mouth, which could have swallowed a calf whole, was drawn in a rictus grin, slobbery red tongue lolling from one side. Teeth like swords. Heavy muzzle. Eyes of burning coal, black and red, no pupils – that head was the worst thing in the world.

Its body might have been the dark itself, wet and dripping and spawned of nightmares. A brutal heaving chest and dear gods but its paws! One blow would fell an ox with scarcely any effort. And it was crouched, and it was grinning, and up it rose.

Leif was struck dumb. Astrid's knife slipped unnoticed from her hand. And in a single bound –

In a single bound, it was past them, leaping so close the rush of air knocked them back, rag dolls flung against the rock wall. Dazed, they turned to follow its flight. As their heads turned, they heard the beat of dreadful wings.

:

Something had risen above the trees on the far side of the valley. A vast black silhouette against the moon's white face, a vaster black shadow in the gorge and on the cliff, the shadow of that wingspan swallowing river and trees and scree and slope. A dread figure rising on the moon, and now it dropped; bearing fire and sword it fell upon the dog, who opened slavering jaws to bay defiance. Then beast and dog met, and their meeting shattered the night, tore a hole upon the earth and rent the sky, and Leif and Astrid, stunned, could only stand and watch the battle of these giants.

The winged beast fell feet first, and kicked out as it came, striking the lunging hound full in the chest. The dog reeled back, jaws knocking together in confusion, and the beast alighted on a spur of rock.

For a moment it was still, and they had their first real glimpse. It was a man, or like a man, thought Astrid, though tall beyond the reach of normal men. White robes swirled over a tight cladding – armour? scales? – of shimmering mail, too bright to quite make out. No longer silhouetted, 'light' now seemed the best way to describe it; it shone hot, harsh white, a stronger light than was ever meant for northern places, and though Astrid longed to see, she had to screen her eyes with her hands.

And anyway it was moving now, a blur of heat and sharp, shimmering edges. With one wing beat it rose aloft and bore down on the hound, sword raised to strike. The sword was fire itself, a living flame, but the dog was ready, twisting aside, wrenching at one wing. A cry came from the beast then, like the screech of an eagle but higher still, and louder, and wilder. It struck out with a leg, and its feet might have been taloned, for it drew blood with that kick – black blood, hot and steaming – and the dog let go its hold and howled.

They came at each other again, both on the ground now. The dog sprang at its throat, looking for a fatal bite, and the beast ducked in low so the dog's teeth scraped its forehead, at the same time driving its flaming sword up, aiming at the Hel-hound's underbelly. Impossibly, the dog ducked its head against the beast's, arching its back into the air and over, somersaulting through the night to land, twisting, behind the beast.

The earth shook with the impact, and the rock split. A gutsome stink of singed dog carried across the water so that Astrid wrinkled up her nose, and now there were fur and feathers massing in the sticky black blood.

With another unearthly scream the beast swung round. Sheathing its sword it dived upon the thrashing dog, still trying to rise from its fall. With grappling arms it seized the hound, and they came up chest to chest, the dog's hind legs scrabbling at the beast's scaled front. With a *crack* and a *whirr* of the threshed night air, the beast's wings began to beat.

And they rose!

That dog must have weighed more than three full-grown male elk, and still the beast's almighty wings bore them into the air. Grunting in pain, the hound made a desperate effort to seize the beast in its jaws, but the teeth slid from the burnished armour. High above the river the titans hovered, dwarfing the valley below.

A third screech, louder than before. And then the beast let go.

The beast let go, and the hound crashed into the waters. The world erupted, river rising high as a mast in one unstoppable wave. Leif and Astrid were dashed against the rock. Had they not already been hard up against it, the impact would surely have killed them. As it was, drenched and sore, they opened their eyes to see the beast, hanging on high, as it drew the burning sword again and gripped it, point down, in both hands.

Then it was in the river and the sword buried to the hilt in the hound. The beast wrenched the blade free and threw back its head. Feet dug into the dying dog, it swung with a mad violence again and again, and the river steamed and hissed. Over the noise of the churning and striking came the hound's death-cry.

Leif felt that the stars might fall at the sorrow of that cry. Astrid, blinking back tears, remembered a dog she had once had that wandered too near the back end of a horse and got its head kicked in. It was the first time she'd thought of it in years.

At last, it was done. The butchered body of the dog sank beneath the waters, lost in the inky murk of its own black blood. The beast rose up with lazy, languid beats – sword dangling from one hand – and then it swivelled its awful head, and looked straight at them.

They both screamed. They couldn't help it: that face, and that gaze, was beyond anything they could handle. To meet those eyes was like being asked to carry a mountain, or being forced to a cliff's edge and told to fly. The face was like a man's, but entirely *other*, inhuman in its weird and perfect beauty. No face should ever be so perfect, but that one was, and it was pure, and serene, and cold.

Blinded with light and fear, they had to close their eyes, even though to do so was beyond awful. Air moved on their faces, and they knew it was landing before them.

Astrid clenched her legs tight together, fighting to control her fear. She might be killed, but she would not die a coward.

The rustle of folding wings. The clink of shifting mail as it bent. That dread face could only be a hand span from their own and, yet, they felt no breath at all. A rasp and a whoosh as the sword was raised to strike, and then –

Nothing. What seemed like seven years of . . . nothing.

Her courage beyond anything she could ever have dreamt before that night, Astrid cracked open one eyelid, no wider than a lash.

The face was right before her. But it wasn't staring back. It was looking lower . . . *it was looking at her neck*.

Judging the best angle to chop at, she thought. But then the beast brought forward one long, slender white finger – tipped with a cruel, curving nail – and touched it to the pendant at her throat.

It screamed, and the noise full in their faces rent their eardrums, and they crumpled, stunned and deafened, and when they struggled to their senses –

It had gone.

A streak of black water, a crevice in the rock. A tarry mass of fur and feathers sticky in the moonlight. And around her neck – she'd barely glanced at it before – a little silver cross, not a Thor's hammer at all.

TWENTY-ONE

ᛏᚹᛅᛀᛏᛁ᛫ᚠ᛫

Next day, pale and red-rimmed, they reported to Thyre in the grove. It was the only place where they could be sure of secrecy. Bumblebees and butterflies laced the heady air beneath the lindens. The queen seemed to be spending ever less time in the hall – shunning even her own bedchamber – and, by the look of her, the baths as well.

'I refuse to take refuge from that pox-ridden Saxon behind my own door! It's nearly midsummer; it befits me to spend time outside, in the sacred places.'

They told her what had happened. 'And here it is,' said Astrid. Bowing her head, she took the silver pendant from round her neck – and winced, as her mother jerked back with distaste plain upon her features.

'Blast that silversmith! I'll see he gets no more custom in Ribe.'

They all looked at the gleaming trinket. The hammer's 'shaft' clearly protruded well above the thin head, forming a cross, rather than a T-shape.

'I think that it's known as a "crucifix",' offered Leif.

'It's known as a swindle, that's what it is,' said Thyre. 'Mixing Christian trinkets in with decent Thor's hammers! Still, it saved your lives. I should never have let you go after that beast, that –'

'Angel,' said Leif.

'Angel?'

'Yes,' said Astrid, 'we've worked it out. The other day, Haralt was asking whether Christians have anything like our Valkyries. Folkmar went on and on – it was all Powers this, Dominions that . . . Haralt lapped it up, of course, he loves that sort of thing. There was a picture in one of Folkmar's "books". Winged avenger, bright light, burning sword – the lot.'

Thyre nodded. 'I remember a little of that. What was it – angels stand somewhere between men and the gods, or "God", I suppose – and are sent to earth to carry messages, or perform important tasks. They sound extremely dangerous. If this is one of them, then it's been sent to do Folkmar's bidding by his god: a tool of destruction in his chubby hands.'

'But the Danes have fought angels before, and won,' said Astrid. 'Ivarr the Boneless drove them out of Norwich, in eastern England, once upon a time.'

'Those were Angles, daughter, not angels,' said Thyre, in some irritation.

Leif stepped in. 'Folkmar's angel: it all makes perfect sense,' he said. 'But that still leaves the hound the angel slew. I'm almost scared to say it, but I think –'

145

'Garm,' said Thyre, with a brisk nod. 'The hound of Hel.'

'Garm?' said Astrid. She'd been raised on terrifying tales of Garm, the watchdog of the underworld. The stories had not lied. But there was one problem with this . . . 'Isn't he supposed to fight the god Tyr, you know, in the final battle of Ragnarok when the world ends?'

Leif nodded. 'Except it seems he's left his post early. He must have been set loose to fight the beast, and swam up through Lake Faarup in the night. But the angel killed him, so he failed.'

He stared at Thyre and Astrid, ashen-faced. 'It's just as the – my trance, I mean – foresaw. If Garm is dead, then Odin's vision cannot come to pass. The future will all change. And there will never be a Ragnarok.'

It had seemed mad, when the stones had warned him that the world might no longer end as had always been foretold, that the thought could *worry* him. But it did. If that certainty, dismal as it was, was removed, then what was there to hold on to? What else might not give way beneath their feet?

Leif saw his own terror reflected in the faces of mother and daughter in front of him – so similar, so scared. The bees, the flowers, the sheltering leaves, seemed sadly out of place.

Thyre was the first to recover from their grim thoughts. 'We cannot fight the angel,' she said. 'If the hound Garm cannot best it, the three of us stand no chance. If only Knut – but no matter . . .'

She jutted out her jaw. 'So we focus on the priest. I think I can hold my husband to the old ways – in the end, Gorm will always listen to my counsel above a stranger's. But if he can't convert the king, Folkmar may try something else. We all know the greatest source of strength around here is –'

'The stones,' said Astrid.

'I'm sure it was the stones that led him here,' said Leif. 'He often spends his nights staring at them.'

A memory flashed like summer lightning. Folkmar asking Haralt about their magic. How had he put it? *'Real power, the power that comes from untold centuries of belief and worship.'*

'Whatever happens,' Thyre said, 'we must keep him from the stones. If he uses their power for his own ends, the old gods will fall. It would be best to drive him out of Jelling altogether. I shall set up a scorn-pole!'

'A storm-pole?' said Astrid.

'Be a dear girl,' said Thyre, in a voice that could have withered the World Tree, 'and run along to the stables? I need you to fetch me a mare – that young grey, perhaps. Oh – and a woodcutter's axe.'

Astrid obeyed. No one could refuse her mother when her mind was made up.

'I take it you at least know what a scorn-pole is?' asked the queen.

Leif nodded. 'A totem that you plant into the ground. You face it at your target, and cut runes into the pole. It asks the earth's spirits to drive the one you're scorning from the land.'

'Very good,' said Thyre. 'Egil Skallagrimsson used just such a pole to drive my husband's first wife, Gunnhild, from Norway – it's a long story. Maybe this will have the same effect. But –' and they looked up at the gentle *clip-clop* of hoofs – 'aren't you forgetting what has to be set on the top of the pole?'

Astrid had returned, leading the most beautiful young mare – soft grey, shaggy mane, huge brown eyes. She stroked her hard, long muzzle as her mother took the axe.

Leif felt sick. 'A scorn-pole's always topped . . . with a mare's head.'

He saw Thyre nod – step forward – saw Astrid back away, eyes wild, mouth open in protest – the axe rise high – and then it all slid away, as he fell into a dead faint.

TWENTY-TWO

ᛏᚤᛏᚢᚱᚾᛃᚤ᛬ᛏᚢᛁᚱ

Thud.

Leif groaned, stirred, turned. *Rustle. Thud.*

And he opened his eyes. He was alone in the grove. It was twilight, still, silent. And a squirrel was dropping acorns on his head.

Seeing him come to, the squirrel came down from the tree – practically poured itself down the trunk – and scurried over to stand by his head. Close to, its needle claws and long, curved teeth were unnerving. But not half so much as its eyes: they were cold, hard stone.

'*Tell us what you've found,*' hissed the squirrel.

ᚦ

'. . . and Thyre's setting up a scorn-pole now,' he finished, 'to set the shaming spirits on the priest.' He had told the stones everything.

'No good,' came the reply. '*The spirits have all fled. All are hiding, all are scared. Garm, the hound of Hel, fallen? Truly, this outlander priest wields the power of a god. His book, his staff, his rituals: so potent. All this, and then he has the angel too.*'

'And yet,' said Leif, 'you want me to stop him?'

'*Yesss,*' they said, and the hiss was long and harsh. '*He must not seize our magic. Or all the North shall fall.*'

'As long as Gorm is king, he has no chance,' said Leif. 'But . . . but if Gorm were to die with Knut abroad . . .'

'*Then Haralt takes the throne.*'

'And Haralt would convert: we'd be undone. Then Folkmar would be free to do his will.'

'*Perhaps.*'

'Perhaps?' said Leif. 'Of course he'd take the Cross!'

'*When we three wrought our spell, in the long-before,*' said the stones, '*we wielded the power of the land. To rule, we knew we needed tree and earth, rock and river.*'

Leif thought about this. 'You mean, that Haralt also needs the land?'

'*Yesss. He cannot rule alone, without the will of this land behind him.*'

'We're talking of the jarls, aren't we?' said Leif.

'*So young,*' they said, '*so quick! Yesss, that is the key. He will only take the step, if he knows the kingdom will go with him.*'

Leif got to his feet, paced about the grove, the little stone-eyed squirrel bounding after him. 'I cannot fight the beast,' he thought, aloud. 'But if the moment were to come for words . . .'

'*We are balanced on the point of the knife,*' came the hiss. The squirrel had leapt to a branch in front of him, on a level with his face. '*The tipping point will come. Then will be the time to use word-magic, to turn the jarls' backs upon the priest. He would be cast out!*'

'Truly, I could best him in a flyting,' Leif said. 'I will challenge him to a war of words.'

Without warning, the squirrel sprang right at his face, so that he reeled backwards; it landed on his shoulder, tiny talons digging into his flesh, drawing blood. The stone-eyed head leant in to his ear, teeth and words both rasping at the lobe. '*The skald who won such a contest, could prove a worthy champion indeed.*'

Leif steadied himself, fighting down the urge to fling the rodent from him. His stomach was still weak from the beheading of the mare. 'You mean . . .'

'*A hero fit to stand up to our scream.*'

And it screeched into his ear. *Thud.*

This time, it was Leif who fell. By the time he picked himself back up, dusting ferns and pine needles from his body, the squirrel was nowhere to be seen.

||

As the stones predicted, no spirits moved against Folkmar. Thyre was furious that her plan had failed, and railed at the priest, calling him a Nithing to his face. This was a deadly insult, enough to start a blood-feud between Danes, but Folkmar only turned a fat smile upon her, saying, 'My apologies; I am not comprehending your language.'

'Perhaps that's half the problem; how can words work on a man who doesn't understand?' Leif said to Astrid. 'It's no surprise that runes don't work on Folkmar, if he has no idea what they mean.'

'Sucks for you,' said Astrid, 'since words are the one thing you're any good at . . .' She had not forgotten how he had fainted in the grove.

He gave her what he hoped was a disdainful look. She gave him what she knew was a well-aimed kick, and then he grabbed for her leg and they were rolling around on the benches . . .

And a hacking, spluttering cough came from the king's bedchamber, and they sat up, saddened.

'It's an age since I tended Father,' said Astrid. They had almost forgotten the king, swept up in events that moved too fast for a failing old man. 'I know – I'll get my harp . . .'

TWENTY-THREE

ᛏᚤᛏᚢᚱᚾ᛫ᚢᛁ᛫ᚦᚱᛁᚱ

Astrid entered her father's room. It felt all wrong. This chamber had once been the centre of her world – an almost sacred place where she rarely dared venture – and from it came power, and law, and gold. But now . . .

It's the smell, she decided. The room had always been dark, and still, and close. But never before had there been this – what was it? – it was familiar . . .

Garm. The bedroom smelt like the breath of the Hel-hound. Rank and rotting. A groan came from the bed.

'Father?' she said. 'King Gorm?'

'Astrid?'

She went to the bed – vast and oaken with curling dragons'-head scrolls at the ends. The silken sheets were rumpled in disorder. Somewhere in their centre, Gorm the Old was trying to sit up.

Astrid hastened to help him, supporting his back and wasted shoulders. It was far too easy. A man of his height should have been much heavier, and Astrid was ashamed.

'My cup,' he croaked, one spindly arm fumbling at the bedside. Her father's wrist was thin, liver-spotted.

She found the cup – small, silver, etched with ribboned beasts – and raised it to his lips. Something clanked in the murky liquid as he drank. Returning it to the chest, Astrid saw a wolf's claw, clinking in the cup. It was an old remedy; the strength of the animal was meant to be passed on to the drinker.

Leif will be pleased, she thought. *My father's clearly no Christian.*

Some of the medicine dribbled down his iron beard and she mopped at it with her sleeve, eyes averted.

'You seem ever more like your mother,' said Gorm, and Astrid blushed.

'Stronger,' he went on. 'More free. More distant.'

She could have cried then.

'Would you like me to play for you, Father?'

He nodded. 'One of the old tunes, Astrid. Make it bright with the hunt and the battle.'

She sat across from him, and took up her harp. A few trial runs and she was away, amid rich chords, the wild deep leaping of the low notes and the high giddy melody that spoke of clashing swords and dancing feet. A series of harsh strums on the off-beat and she was there, in the fire and the fury, and Gorm was there too, his clouded white eyes fixed on the direction of the music, stiff old fingers beating almost in time to the tune.

At last she paused, worried she had taken him too far.

'Play on, shield maiden,' he said. 'I have your back.' He grinned a wolf's grin, and she went on. His whole upper body was swaying with the rhythm now, and when at last she laid down the harp, fingers smarting, there were tears on both their faces.

'Come, daughter,' he said, and held out an arm.

Astrid crept into his embrace, really worried now. He had not held her like this in years.

'Daughter, I stand so near Valhalla's doors that I can hear the shouts and smell the roasting-spit. But even now, with my face turned to Odin's kingdom, I sense the troubles of my own at my back.'

She burrowed closer into his side, nose scrunched bravely against the smell of him.

'At such a time, I would have my heir near me, and I know Thyre feels Knut's lack sorely. He's a worthy son, and if he wrests the rule of Dublin from Olaf the Sure-Shod, why, his fame might even surpass mine! A father could not wish for more . . .'

'. . . But?' said Astrid.

'But for all that, it sometimes seems a pity that he, not Haralt, is to sit in my throne after me.'

'Haralt?' Oh, the things she could tell him about her brother!

Gorm chuckled, though the effort cost him much. 'He's not much loved by his own blood, is he? But then, the flock does not love the dog. Haralt may not have the beard of a true king, but he has the head, and I think the heart too.'

Gorm's voice was slow and rasping. 'All this fussing over

155

faith – I think he knows what he's about. It might be well for this land if its next king rules with the Cross as well as the sword.'

'But if Haralt was allowed, he'd wipe out all the old ways!'

'I've been listening to his talk with the priest. He is ambitious. Haralt wants to build bridges – not just with Germany, but real bridges of wood, even of stone. He talks of forts . . . This land wants taming, Astrid; it's too wild, too free. Your mother's people across the water, in the border lands, they're little better than wolves, and it'll take more than a few berserkers to keep them in order. Odin knows I did some terrible things in my youth, but I'd do them again, and those who come after me may well have to, if they are to keep hold of my kingdom.'

'Terrible things?'

'Too terrible even for your bloodthirsty ears, Astrid. My point is, you may not love your brother – and I'd never ask you to *like* him – but don't fight him. He has our family's interests at heart. And nothing good comes of it when one's children quarrel.'

Astrid's mouth was a hard line.

Gorm sighed. 'Try, anyway, just a little. And, Astrid, I've a second thing to tell you – a secret. Not even your mother must know.'

Gorm smiled his wolf's head smile, and there was something cracked and crazy in it.

'I've gone blind!' he said.

TWENTY-FOUR

ᛏᚢᛏᚢᛚᚾ:ᛉᚢ:ᚠᛁᚼᚱᛁᚱ

The summer died in indecision; autumn's splendid rot set in. The world was streaked rust-red and gold, fruits and berries tumbling onto the long trestle tables. The harvest was brought in, the blindness of the king leaked out. Stubbled fields bled into browning forests. The nights drew cold. Folkmar's waddle was becoming a swagger; Leif practised speeches for a flyting; no birds sang. Men walked in fear of what was to come, and what might not, and it was rumoured Gorm the Old would not last another winter.

Thyre's face was a storm cloud in these days, as more and more of the Thor's hammers vanished from around necks, melted into coinage or even recast into true crosses. Haralt sent for engineers from Hamburg, to chart the marshes where the trolls still mourned and to see about building a bridge there.

Astrid was not sleeping well, out in the stables. Both her parents falling apart; her favourite brother risking his

157

life across the ocean; the terror of Hellir, the gorge, and Folkmar's wandering fingers – it was no surprise, she told herself, that she could imagine the sound of the angel, landing on the stable roof.

Soft wing beats. A creak of timbers. Slow pacing.

She turned over, trying to ignore the sounds her over-wrought mind must be imagining.

Another creak; a scatter of fallen dust and splinters across her upturned cheek.

After all, it made no sense for the angel to be here: it was on a mission to kill pagan creatures, things of magic. And there was nothing of that sort here.

A jolt. A thud. Except for . . .

A sudden flurry of sounds, a high skittering above; three jarring strides and a crash of rent wood. Above it all, the thinnest, smallest squeal and then a deafening shriek of triumph.

Except for . . .

'Nisse!' she screamed. In a blur of terror Astrid leapt from the bed, groped for flint and tinder, struck a light. The din of the departing angel as it rose up from the roof was all around her. And at the foot of the bed lay a tiny, childlike figure, crumpled from its fall. It was the first time she'd actually seen him.

There was so little blood.

Astrid buried Nisse in the stable, the packed, hard earth moistened by her tears. *If the tipping point is coming*, she thought, *and all this will be ended, then let it come soon.* Though, had she drunk from Mimir's well of wisdom and seen what *was* to come, she would have wished those words unsaid.

158

One morning, Gorm stirred from his bed, and set the whole of Jelling scurrying.

'What are the men about?' Astrid asked her mother, relieved that something was happening.

'They are set to start reshaping the mound,' said Thyre, and her words were as rocks on a stormy headland.

'What, the old burial mound beside the Yelling Stones? But why?'

And then Astrid bit her lip, afraid of the answer.

'Your father . . . Your father's thoughts have turned to the hereafter,' said Thyre. She hid her face for a moment. 'At least we need not fear his following Christ! Gorm the Old will go to his grave Odin's man.' And then she stalked off, overcome.

Outside, a gale whipped men's cloaks and hair about their faces, and made it hard to see. Shielding her eyes, Astrid bent into the winter wind and ran out to the stones. Beyond them she saw her father, wrapped in wolf skins, supported on either side, and gesturing here and there to warriors-turned-workmen. They brought shovel and adze, and felled trees in the forest, and all the time King Gorm stood erect in the wind, grey and grim as a standing stone himself, and, blind though he was, directed the digging of his own grave.

ᚦ

All the villages for days' travel around sent men to help with the mound's enlargement – it was not as if they had a choice. Jarl Tofi, the man Knut had called a sissy, came in person with a score of workers from Baekke. He sat stone-faced at Thyre's side, watching the digging and laying and turfing. Gorm was set on its being finished before the first snows fell.

And finished it was. As the first flurries came in from the west, wet and driving and sludgy white, they fell upon an immense and green-turfed mound, dwarfing the hall. Tools were packed and labourers ran home, to reach their firesides and families before the worst of the snow hit.

'Perhaps now we can all forget this folly and start thinking about our family's *actual* future?' said Haralt, at dinner. 'There is the question of Astrid's marriage, for instance.'

Outside, a blizzard was growing. Haralt raised his voice above it. 'I have been having thoughts on that matter. It is in our best interests to strengthen Danish ties to the Saxon court. At this very table, we have a representative –'

Astrid and Thyre both opened their mouths to shout Haralt down. Then they closed them again. Haralt too tailed off. Everyone was suddenly silent.

Someone was hammering on the doors of the hall.

|

'Who comes calling at such a time, and in this weather?' Haralt cried.

'Oh for Thor's sake, someone open the accursed door,' snapped Thyre.

Two men leapt to the task. As soon as the massive oak bar was raised, the gale flung the doors apart, knocking the men to the ground.

All eyes peered against the swirling white. All faces felt the chill. The hall fires guttered and dwindled with the blast. And in came a man.

He was broken, and bent, and swaddled up against the snow with moulting piles of bloodied bearskin. His face was a web of scars. His eyes were sunken pits, and his hands . . . his hands . . .

'Weland!' cried Thyre. Everyone rose to get a better look at the one-time warrior.

'What? Our smith returned?!'

'Come in, Weland, come and get warm!'

'What brings you back alone, man?'

'How fares Knut?'

But Thyre stood in silence, both hands before her mouth. She eyed Weland as if he were a ghost.

Slowly, everyone in the hall realised that something was very, very wrong. The cries of greeting ebbed away into awful silence. No one could move; no one save that shambling figure, edging up towards the stricken queen.

And in that silence, another door banged behind her, and Gorm the Old fumbled his way from his bed to stand before his throne. He raised two trembling, skeleton's hands above his head. And he stared, unseeing, straight at Weland, and he cried out, in a voice like coffins toppling open, 'My son Knut is dead!'

TWENTY-FIVE

ᛏᚢᛏᚢᚱᛁᚤᚠᛁᛏ

Only two people were still. Weland, sunk to the floor, the centre of a swarm of people, all asking the same question. And Thyre, frozen on the dais, hands still before her mouth.

Below her, all was chaos. Half the hall went to Weland; the other half surged around the blind king. Hands stretched before him, Gorm shuffled from the high table down to the hall floor. He spoke sharply to the first men to reach him, who bowed, backed away, and then darted past Thyre into the king's bedchamber.

Astrid ran towards Weland. She could hear snatches of his speech amid the din. 'Dublin –' 'ambush –' 'an arrow –' 'dead –' 'no other survivors.'

A wolf had hold of her heart, and was gnawing it to pieces.

Gorm meanwhile never paused, treading a straight path towards the doors, which still swung open, unheeded. 'Stand back,' he called. 'I am still your king.' A wary circle formed around him.

He never glanced at the prone Weland, never turned his head, even to acknowledge the return of the runners. One bore his sword – the Toledo blade Leif had given him – and placed it in the king's right hand. Somehow he took its weight. The other carried, hooded on his arm, the king's eagle, Hreggskornir; it hopped to the king's left shoulder. Two more men walked behind, and between them was a chest – ornate, and heavy, to judge from the bowing of their backs.

Gorm's grey gown billowed behind him in the face of the winter blast. His beard whipped up and the eagle spread its wings. Someone had slipped its hood and now it raised its beak, cawing in defiance of any who dared approach. There were three stuttering fires lit down the length of that great hall, and as the awful figure passed, each in turn went out.

One. Two. Three. Snuffed like candles when Gorm the Old went by.

'Have the doors closed,' a white-faced Haralt muttered to Arinbjorn. 'This has gone far enough.'

The old Norwegian sent four men racing for the doors, but the wind rose as they bent to their task, huge icy fists dashing them back against the walls.

As Gorm approached the winds parted, closing on his tall grey frame and slamming the doors shut behind him. Now men ran to wrestle them open again, hauling the massive panels back and rushing out into the racing white night, after the blind king. Leif and Astrid slipped between them. Somewhere, a horse whinnied.

Incredibly, Gorm was mounted, sword raised in his right hand, eagle on his left wrist, the reins, let loose, tugged about by the wind. Behind him in the saddle was lashed the heavy chest. The horse was huge, and grey, and old, and their backs were turned to the milling crowd.

'Hear me, old friends,' cried the king. Somehow they knew the words were meant, not for any person there, but for the stones themselves.

'All my life, I have offered you the blood of my sacrifices. In living, you have made me great! Do not fail me in my death!'

Without a glance, the king touched his heels to the horse's flanks, and the beast cantered straight between the Yelling Stones.

An almighty thunderclap sprawled the watchers, and the horse reared up at the stones' centre. Lightning flashed from between the stones; shot out to strike the newly raised earthwork.

For a moment, all were blinded, deafened, struck by the force of the lightning crack.

And then it was quiet, and the wind died, and the horse trotted calmly north. The great mound opened before the rider. The king rode into the mound, and the mound closed upon him.

People picked themselves up. Gorm the Old had gone. He had ridden into his own grave, and it had welcomed him.

:

Astrid's eyes, impossibly, were dry as she fled the crowd and ran back into the horrid smoky press of the hall. Scrabbling about on the bench, she drew her harp from a bundle of cloaks.

'Play on, shield maiden,' her father had said. *'I have your back.'*

'I'll never play again,' she said, and flung it in the fire. The strings snapped and the bridge cracked; greedy flames ate up the wood.

Leif looked from her, to the fire, to the dais where Thyre still stood, unmoving. And what was he meant to do *now*?

ᚴ

Night, and the gale returned with the dark. Ice lashed at Leif's exposed cheeks as, in desperation, he strode out to the stones. 'What would you have me do, you useless rocks?' he shouted, words whipped away into the black.

Not even an echo greeted his words.

For a moment, he stood before them, thwarted. And then he stepped forward.

A monstrous adder reared up in his path, uncoiling from the foot of the nearest stone. It rose as high as his waist, jaws agape, and Leif staggered back. Its eyes were dead grey stone, and now it swayed before him, fixing those eyes on his own.

'Now is the time: the tipping point is come! The jarls will gather here to mourn their king, and choose his successor.'

'Haralt.'

'*Haralt. He and the priest will seek to turn their heads. You must strike now – talk to these men, draw first blood!*'

Leif shook his head. 'That isn't what I meant. I meant, what can I do to help Astrid?'

'*Tcha!*' The snake shot its head at him; reared higher. '*Forget the girl. She is but flesh. Now is the moment for word-magic, to conquer fate, to wield true power!*'

'No.'

'*No?! You dare oppose our will, boy?*'

'You all say I'm the one who makes the choices.' And he remembered the words of the witch-rider. '*Three choices. The first will be right.*' It was some comfort. 'So Folkmar and the flyting can go hang. I make my first choice, and I choose my friend.'

'*Fool!*' spat the adder. '*If we fall to the priest, then you fall too. Your words, your magic, they are pagan tools. They'll kill you as a heathen! As a witch like us!*'

'And yet for all that, I will choose my friend.'

In a fury, the adder struck.

'Rope,' said Leif, with a curl of his lip, and the snake fell, harmless, to the ground. Leif turned on his heel, an idea burning in his mind. Astrid needed him. That was all that mattered now.

TWENTY-SIX

ᛏᚹᛁᚾᛏᛁᛁᛦ᛬ᛋᛁᛈᛋ

The snow fell and fell, and skiers as well as riders were sent
to call in the jarls of Jylland. As the winter worsened they
struggled in, from farmsteads and villages, from fjord and
field, Ribe and Hedeby, Viborg and Aarhus, from Lindholm
and Vorbasse and even Odense, for the crossing was still
makeable and the ice had not yet set in.

They came on hardy winter ponies, they came in longships
drawn up down at Vejle Fjord. They even came in sledges.
But they would not come from further east, from Lejre and
Ringsted, Roskilde and Uppaakra, and this was bad news
for Thyre, for they were her people who were cut off by
the winter. The men of Jylland were the true Danes, fat and
rich. They would follow Haralt's example if they thought
there was enough in it for them.

Leif saw them pass him on the roads – Jarl Ari and Jarl
Eyvind, and Jarl Tofi Ravnsson, now sporting a sky-blue
cloak over his snow-white tunic. They paid him no mind, a

boy on a horse, just another rider sent to call them to Gorm's mourning. And he scarce noticed them, so taken up was he with his purpose – and with trying to stay on Hestur's back.

'This is the hardest magic I've tried yet,' he whispered to the horse. 'I've spurned the stones and left Jelling for this; it's going to take blood, and fire, and time. So, please try not to dump me in the snow?'

Hestur whinnied, halting as gently as he could for the strange boy on his back. Leif wobbled, peering through the falling white. Before them roared the sea, grey and cold and heavy. The sea had something Leif wanted, and the sea always asked a price.

Leif shook his head. 'You will ever ask us for the same thing,' he said to the sea. He drew a knife, and, holding out his hands above the roaring surf, snicked the tip of the thumb, and each finger, of his left hand, so the blood ran free, whipped away into the hungry water.

He grimaced as he bandaged the now-useless hand. But before him on the broad whiteness of beach, the sea had thrown up five slick lumps of amber. The first of six bargains had been struck.

Ↄ

Astrid sat before the fire that had eaten up her harp, and stared into the flames. The fire was warm; she knew that to be true. But she felt – nothing.

Not grief. Not pain. Nothing. Nothing, nothing, nothing.
Did she cry? She couldn't tell.
Nothing.

᛭

Leif's pack bulged. He had spoken to the sea, to alder trees, to a store of last season's flax, and struck bargains with them all. He had lit warming fires for a hive of bees in return for their wax. And now he could return to Jelling, where his last two deals would be made.

'I need something from you as well, Hestur,' he said. 'Strings wound from hair plucked from a stallion's tail.'

The horse snorted, bucked a little. Leif leant near to its ear, and whispered what he needed it for. Hestur relaxed, and the price he asked came clear into Leif's mind.

A good, hot mash.

ᛀ

A part of Astrid's mind wondered where Leif was. This was the time, she knew, when he needed to act.

The gathering jarls would elect Haralt as the new king. If he had their backing, her brother – her *only* brother – would take the Cross and have the whole kingdom converted. Folkmar would be free to seize the power of the Yelling Stones, and the old gods would fall. Probably, she thought, Haralt's first act as a Christian king would be to marry her off to Folkmar. And she stopped short of imagining what *that* would mean.

But if Folkmar was humiliated in front of all these men – if someone with the wit and skill of Leif could best him with words – then Haralt would never dare become a Christian.

No Dane would take on such embarrassment willingly, least of all the king.

They knew this, the prince and the priest. That was why they were walking among the new arrivals, clasping hands, embracing, giving gifts. Stealing a march on any challenger.

So why wasn't Leif here, doing the same thing?

A part of her wondered this.

But mostly, she just stared at the fire. She felt nothing.

Leif slipped into Folkmar's room, swinging shut the loose plank behind him. Once, that plank had swung open to reveal Astrid. The world had been younger then, and happier.

A low-burning oil lamp shone dim on gold. At least Knut, who had died a Viking raider, would have approved, as Leif stuffed the ornate, gilded candlestick into his sack. He had all the pieces. Now, time for the real magic.

On the other side of the door, the hall hummed with talk. Folkmar was busy making important friends. To all those men, Leif was no one: friendless, ally-less. Of all his six bargains, this had been the highest price by far.

ᚼ

Astrid was still staring, into the fire. If she looked hard enough, she might make them out among the flames – father and brother, half her family, taken from her in one impossible instant.

170

'Astrid?' It was Leif. 'I have something for you. A gift I made.'

For the first time in what seemed like forever, she looked up. He seemed older, wilder, thinner. His left hand was a mass of red rags. In his right, he held something out to her.

It was a harp.

TWENTY-SEVEN

ᛏᚾᛏᚢᚱᚾ᛬ᛉᚠ᛬ᛋᛁᛏᚾ

The instrument he held was small, simple, shaped like a fan, or a quiver, or a horn. A rounded wooden butt blossomed into a backboard, long and slim, a single piece of alder wood widening to a scroll and a slant. Shined with beeswax, oiled with flaxseed. It was of a size to be laid across her knees, and had five horsehair strings that fanned out with the wood, raised above the surface, pegged with amber. The strings were stretched across a slim bar of gold.

'I told you my grandmother was a Lapp,' he said. 'From Finland. She had one of these; they call these instruments "kanteles". And they say there's magic in them, that they heal a heart. That they're best made when one you love has died, for part of them lives on between its strings.'

He paused, uncertain. 'I didn't really know how your harp looked. This was the best that I could do instead . . .'

She was looking at him very strangely. He knew what he was meant to say – that he was sorry for her loss, that he understood how badly she felt, that it would get better, in time – and couldn't say a word of it. So he held out the honeyed, smooth-grained harp, and hoped that she would take it.

Inside Astrid, something was unfurling. From stony, frozen depths it stirred, creeping upwards, touching her with its teeth and claws. Where it touched, she felt again: felt grief, and loss, and pain. *At last*. This, she supposed, was love. It hurt. And that was good.

So she reached up, and took the harp. Laid it in her lap, stroking it as if it were a cat, not yet daring to pluck a string.

'It has no tuning key,' she said, surprised. They were the first words she'd spoken in several days.

'It shouldn't need one. All the strings serve you.'

He pointed to the middle of the five strings. 'That one especially will change at will: if you're happy, the string will tighten up. And if you're sad, it slackens, like a back.'

There were so many questions to ask, she thought. But then, he looked so very, very tired.

'Play, Astrid,' he said. 'Just play.'

So she did. She learnt her way round the five strings, teasing out chords. The first, the fourth, the fifth string – and all heads in the hall turned at the sound of that expectant, hopeful clutch of notes.

First, *third* and fifth, and listeners stiffened as the major chord followed, the two together sounding like a calm but murky sea, something shifting under the waters.

She plucked the same three strings, but now the third slackened of its own accord, the minor note wrenching the whole sound into strife. She followed, fingers nimbling, with first, second, fifth, then first, first again and fifth, and the sequence spoke of earth and grave and the certainty of darkness.

Those five chords, over and over again. Shovel after shovel of dank soil, heaped upon hope, heaped upon joy.

No one was speaking. The jarls had all sunk down upon the benches, heads cast low. Tofi of Baekke was already weeping loudly as the music filled the hall. It was less the sound of sadness than despair.

Something struck Leif. If Astrid could conjure such sadness from these strings that it broke men's hearts, then maybe it could turn their heads. Maybe this would be the way to beat Folkmar.

And in that case, he wouldn't have thrown everything away by his choice to make the harp. He would have helped Astrid, *and* saved the north lands. He could have both, couldn't he?

Couldn't he?

Astrid's sequence suddenly jarred, both third and fifth strings going slack, and the eerie, diminished chord stirred the slumped listeners so they shifted in their seats. And now she began a new tune, lighter, with more movement, and this one was the sound of tears itself.

Everyone was crying now. And Leif really dared to hope, that his choice had been the right one, not just for Astrid, but for the land as well.

Even Folkmar was crying. 'Beautiful,' he said, wiping tears from his fat eyes. 'Beautiful!' He waddled across to Astrid, laying one heavy hand on her shoulder. With the other, he pawed at her hair, lovingly. She shuddered, trapped by the weight of him.

And then he turned to the silent jarls. 'It is a miracle,' he said. 'A miracle. That the girl should play like this, on today of all days.'

'What day, bishop?' said Haralt, coming back to his normal self.

'Why, it is November the twenty-second, Saint Cecilia's day. She who watches over all the musicians; she who died with a song on her lips praising Our Lord, and is now by His side in Heaven! It is Saint Cecilia who is making this music so beautiful!' And his piggy eyes shone with emotion.

All around, jarls were nodding.

Oh skita, thought Leif.

TWENTY-EIGHT

ᛏᚢᚢᚱᚾᛁᚠᛁᛏ

'And thus Haralt, son of Gorm, is hereby elected king over us, the Danes, and over the people of the Dane-mark, and all people of such lands as shall submit to his authority by sword or by oath. Come forward, Haralt, son of Gorm, in the sight of these people, before the Yelling Stones, and receive this earth, to swear to it your love and protection.'

Haralt came forth from the crowd and took the snowy clod of soil in his right hand. Dumbly, he sketched the sign of Thor over the earth, eyes downcast.

'I swear it,' he murmured.

'Then it is done.'

|

Haralt ordered that his new throne – beech wood, square and massive – be set halfway up the mound, where he sat in state above everyone. Each jarl stepped forward to

176

swear his own oath to the new king.

When this too was done, Haralt raised his voice. 'Now for my first act as king. Bishop Folkmar here, who is known to you all, has told me much of Christ, the god of the Germans, Franks and English, and also of the Romans and the Emperor at Miklagard. And so, not only for my own sake, or for all of your sakes, but also out of love for my great father Gorm, whose spirit I wish to see at peace, I am of a mind to renounce the old gods, and pledge myself to Christ.'

The crowd around the stones quivered. They had expected this – but you can see a storm coming, and it will still blow your house down.

Astrid had lost Leif in the throng. Still clutching her harp as if it really did contain the spirits of her father and brother, she peered about. This was the moment. The tipping point. Surely he would say something now?

A figure broke free with a swish of white wool, arm raised. Astrid blinked. It was Jarl Tofi.

'Wait,' he said. 'Do my ears deceive me? Has the king to whom I've just sworn my oath – an oath witnessed by these very stones, taken in the name of Odin, Thor and Frey – I say again, has this king of mine just forsaken everything that made my oath binding?'

He flashed a brilliant smile all around. 'Because it seems to me, that the king who would take such a spectacular risk must either be as brave as Sigurd . . . or the greatest fool and blockhead in the North!'

Haralt coloured, as gasps ran round the throng. 'I would not presume,' he said, 'to chance the luck of the kingdom without believing the change to be for the better –'

'Aye,' shouted Tofi, 'that's the point, isn't it? Belief? And I for one will not be persuaded of the worth of that fat Saxon's Christ –' he flapped a hand dismissively at Folkmar – 'without putting it to the test. Let's have a flyting!'

'A flyting!' The cry was taken up all around. Astrid could see her mother, pale and wan, looking ten years older, but managing to smile. She must have put Tofi up to this . . .

'Where's the skald? He'll make the case for the old gods!' But half of those shouting were Haralt's men, Astrid realised.

'Bring the boy forward; we'll hear them, then decide!'

A grim certainty settled on her: whatever Leif said now, the result had been fixed at those meetings in the hall. That was why Haralt was letting the crowd have its say – he knew where their loyalties lay already. Folkmar would win, by fair means or foul.

And Leif emerged, small and thin between all those powerful men. A hush descended.

Leif's mouth was dry as a salt pit in summer. His palms itched in anticipation. So, words were the only thing he was good at, were they? Time to find out.

At last.

'As this court's skald, I will accept this test: I challenge Folkmar in the old gods' names.' His eyes met the priest's. 'But not to a flyting. That game's been rigged. I have in mind a different ordeal.'

Haralt's blue eyes were hard as glass. 'You test my patience, boy; get on with it.'

But now Folkmar waddled out next to Leif. Astrid watched his face, and his hand. It was opening and closing; he was practically panting with desire. Beside him, Leif was grinning. He looked as mad as a fox.

For a moment she was confused.

Leif and Folkmar spoke together. 'The two of us will stand between the stones.'

And then she understood.

Astrid had been but a small child when Bragi had stood on that very spot at midsummer. A girl of seven. She had seen the flames, seen the shattered, twisted, blackened body. And she had stood there again on a cold spring night, and laughed at the arrogance of a strange and wonderful boy. And a third time, when Folkmar had first arrived, and stared at the Yelling Stones with the hunger of winter.

'But this is madness!' she cried, blundering forward. And, inside, she screamed, *This is my fault!*

If Leif hadn't chosen to make her a harp, he would have been ready; he could have won the flyting. He wouldn't have had to try this – this *stupid* gesture . . .

Oh, it was just like him!

'Stop,' she shouted again.

But it was too late.

Leif and Folkmar strode as one into the stone circle. Together they entered. And together . . . they vanished.

TWENTY-NINE

ᛏᛁᛏᚢᛍᛁ·ᚼ�·ᚼᛁᚾ

He was being spun like a leaf in the gale. In the hurricane. There was the dry rushing round him, and he bashed into the priest's soft body but he never even knew.

In his ears was the yell.

It was all on one note, at three pitches, impossibly high, impossibly low; savage, bloody, and old beyond counting.

It filled his ears, his head, his whole being; shook him through to bursting. His ears began to bleed.

He was *in* that scream. It was thunder and lightning, waterfall and landslide, wolf's howl, boar's squeal, and eagle's piercing cry. Leif could feel it ripping him to pieces.

For a time beyond reckoning, there was nothing in the world but that scream. And then, from somewhere, there came a memory. Not of an image, of a touch, of a smell. But of a tune. Yesterday's tune; the tune of Astrid's heart. The notes she had played rose up, unbidden, and thrummed louder and louder within him till they were louder than the yell.

Next to Astrid's song, the yell left him cold. He could handle it.

†

Outside the circle, the Danes milled about in shock.

'Do we wait?' someone said.

Astrid bit her lip.

'They've just . . . they've just *gone*.'

Crazily, uselessly, Leif had shut his eyes against the sound of the stones – *and* his mouth, and curled his toes, clenched his fists. It had done no good. But now he had the song to hold on to, and he could relax his body, and open his eyes.

The first thing he saw was Folkmar. The priest's own eyes were still scrunched tight. He was passing a length of knotted rope through and through his hands, murmuring words lost in the savage noise. He seemed to have found his own way of coping. Leif was impressed.

The second thing he noticed was that they hadn't moved – they were still standing together inside the circle. Only, Jelling itself was gone. The hall, the mound, and every living person except the two of them – gone. Instead on every side there stretched a forest, thick and dark and wild and breathing. The light itself was wan, thin, barely there. A mist rose from the dank green grass. It was dawn, or the moment just before.

The third thing, which he realised just a little too late, was that the two stones he could see, didn't look like stones any more. In the dim, spider-webbed light, they looked far more like – like what exactly? Trolls? Witches? Both? It was hard to tell, for they wore their hair long to their toes.

Anyway, that was what explained the growing pain in both his shoulders, where the third sister held him fast with taloned fingers.

↑

If he came out of this alive, Leif promised himself, he would be earning his supper with the story till his hair turned grey.

Then he tried to struggle free of those claws, but his left hand was still bandaged and useless, and the witch-sister – the short, stout one – was far stronger than him. It was some small comfort to see Folkmar just as helpless in the clutches of the long, lean sister. He tried to think. This wasn't like before, when they'd spoken through a vessel. This was the real thing. Perhaps he had been wrong to defy them; perhaps this could all have been so much easier. Oh if only the scream would *stop*, he could clear his head . . .

The scream. That was it.

The chief sister, who dwarfed even Folkmar, was staring straight at him, mouth wide open in the awful yell. But her eyes were asking a question.

Leif focused on the scream. For the first time, there seemed to be words in it. Maybe no one but a skald would have noticed the tiny ripplings of sound for what they were. It

182

was like picking snowflakes from a blizzard, droplets from a torrent. If he tried really, really hard, he could fish the words from the yell's rush.

'You . . . spurned . . . us,' the words said. '*But still you dare to come.*'

He nodded.

'*You are brave. Headstrong. Until now, you were weak. You did our will, and there is no honour in being anyone's thrall, even ours. But now . . . you are perhaps a worthy champion.*'

Leif almost laughed at this. It *had* been the right choice. Still, he wasn't ready to trust them yet. There had to be a catch. 'But you have waited here a thousand years. Surely, others have been brave before me?'

'*None so quick, none so gifted. None so humble as to bring a worthy offering. The last to try brought us nothing.*'

'"The last to try" – you mean Bragi?' he said, and then, 'What offering?' But the word stream flowed on, growing faster.

'*Let us show you,*' they said. '*Let us show you what such power will bring.*'

And again he was spinning, caught up in a storm. The needling claws never slackened their grip on his shoulders, but what he saw before him flickered and shifted like a guttering flame.

The dark, ancient forest was gone. Now, he was looking at the great hall, from an unfamiliar position. He was in Gorm's old ash throne. Astrid sat at his right. Before him on the floor, Haralt and Tofi bent their heads. With them were others whose names shimmered in his head. Haakon of Norway. Bjorn and Emund, kings of Sweden. The lords of the North, paying *him* homage.

The image blurred, faded. Blinking, Leif saw himself on the shore of an unknown country. In the distance, fumes rose out of the black and red earth. *Iceland*. A man was strolling towards him, arms spread in welcome, the glow of respect in his eyes. From the man's enormous size and dark colouring, Leif knew him to be his hero – Egil Skallagrimsson, the greatest skald alive.

The scene changed again, and now Leif was watching from horseback as men – *his* men – poured in an unstoppable flood upon a shining town many times the size of Hedeby. Screaming townspeople fled to the shelter of a great stone church. He spoke a word and its walls crumbled. He spoke again and Hamburg was his.

'*None will stand before the power of your voice*,' they said.

Now vision crowded upon vision, as he strode across Germany, England, Ireland, and at his side was a merry throng. A laughing man upon a boar; two beautiful women, one in a chariot drawn by cats, one with hair of pure gold; the thunderer himself, swinging his hammer; and an old, old man, leaning on a staff, the brim of his hat tugged low over his one good eye. He walked across the world, and the gods walked with him.

'*It will all be yours.*'

He was back in the circle of sisters, and the deep green forest sighed and heaved. Unseen shapes writhed and rustled among the trees. This place must be Jelling as *they* had known it – the wilderness where they had wrought the spell, the moment before they turned to stone.

He was all at once aware of a cold weight in his right hand. Looking down, Leif saw he was holding a knife.

'*Make the offering*,' they said. '*Make the offering, and end this fight.*'

He looked around, confused. There was nothing but himself, the three sisters . . . and Folkmar, deaf to their words, unseeing, still stammering through his prayers.

And he understood.

THIRTY

ᚦᚱᛁᛦ·ᛏᛁᚠᛦ

The second choice was upon him. *'Three choices,'* the witch-rider had said. *'The first will be right. And the others . . . will be wrong.'* The first choice had ended up bringing him here, when he made the harp and forsook the flyting. But that choice had been simple. This one was not.

There were words in the yell once more.

'It will be so easy,' they said. *'What is a man, when the knife slips in, but flesh and blood?'*

Flesh and blood. Flesh . . . blood . . .

He looked at the priest. So soft. So afraid. So dangerous.

He had a duty to the trolls. To Astrid's Nisse. To a whole world he held dear, of gods and spirits, words and magic. A world that the priest would destroy if he let him go.

A world that, now and ever, had its wergild: its blood-price. A world bought every year by sacrifice to hungry gods. Bought by the blood of birds, rams, oxen – by the slaughter of gentle grey mares. Folkmar's world, he knew, had been saved by the blood-price of *his* god, by Christ's self-sacrifice. Why shouldn't Leif's world be saved by the sacrifice of Folkmar?

He held up the blade. So sharp it almost sang. Folkmar was helpless, unaware – he wouldn't feel a thing.

'No,' he said, and dropped the knife. It was swallowed by the tall grass.

'*Then our use for you is at an end,*' came the words. '*Both of you shall die.*'

The scream grew louder, monstrously louder, as the sisters closed for the kill. With his one good hand Leif groped behind him, searching for his captor's eyes. Sharp teeth closed upon his fingers, and he felt the splintering of bone.

His skin prickled, burnt, blistered with sound. The last thing he saw as he fell into darkness was Folkmar, eyes open, arms raised high. Even now, Folkmar believed that his god would save him.

'Phanuel!' the priest called.

The angel fell from the clear dawn sky, the rush of air knocking Leif down. A new cry arose amid mad hacking and rending as the angel tore into the sister that held Folkmar, feet and teeth ripping, wielding the burning sword.

But Leif was a dumb, terrified beast, flames taking hold, and the *very* last two things he knew were red – flame red – and black.

†

Astrid had just decided to stop blaming herself, when it happened. She hadn't really forced Leif into this at all. It had been what he'd wanted, since the beginning, just as much as Folkmar: to test himself against the stones.

So she would blame *him* instead. In fact, when she got hold of him, she'd –

And Leif fell out from between the Yelling Stones, a human candle; fell with a moan and a spluttering hiss into the heaped snow. She ran to him at once, and at once was shoved aside, as the court healer – a man named Hrafn – barrelled his way through the crowd.

'Get his rags off,' Hrafn ordered, and Astrid pulled at his tattered, smoking tunic. Some of his skin stuck to the weave as she tugged, and she winced, fearing his pain, but Leif never moved. He was gone from her, gone far, far away.

'You can do nothing more now, girl; leave him with me,' said Hrafn, not unkindly. He and Kolga, his assistant, pulled Leif's limp body aside, sluicing it with snow, then set to laying pads over the worst of the burns. Astrid smelt violets as they applied the poultices – a strangely sweet scent, amid so much horror.

Odin, Christ, whoever, I don't care, she thought. *If you can hear me, then please. Don't take him too.*

†

But now more was happening behind her. Astrid wheeled round to see Folkmar loom out of the circle. Then there was a rush of hot, desert wind, and everyone blinked at the sudden glare.

The angel was there, among them, a brilliant whirl of light and fury, and all the Danes saw it swing its sword. The blade sheered through the thinnest of the Yelling Stones as if it were a hollow log.

The stone shattered, exploded, a hundred shards flung wide. They all hurled themselves to the ground as chunks of rock whizzed overhead. And then there was total horror, because the stone circle was broken, and the yell itself came free.

They all heard it, that long-frozen scream, crashing outwards like an ocean wave, echoing and re-echoing off the mound and off the hall, pummelling the listeners, bludgeoning their bodies against the ground.

Haralt himself, halfway up the mound, was toppled off his throne by the sheer power of the noise. He scurried back to his seat, glancing about to make sure that no one had seen.

Astrid's nose was bleeding. The blood ran across her stone-blasted face, tickling her, but she never thought of wiping it away. Her hands were clapped fast over her ears.

At last the yell rose up from that place like a vast flock of birds, and like a flock it broke, and circled, and fled upon the winter air. Then it was gone, and the Danes helped each other to their feet.

Folkmar stood implacably before them, alone again. No one had seen the angel leave. None could even be quite sure of what they had just seen. But a miracle had happened, they were sure of that, and the Yelling Stones were broken.

THIRTY-ONE

ᚠᚱᛁᚱ:ᛏᛁᚠᛁᚱ:ᛁᛏ

Haralt was baptised at once, in a barrel of heated water. Dressed only in a shift, he stepped in up to his waist, letting Folkmar sprinkle him with droplets, pass his hands about and speak still more Latin. It was not unlike a child's naming ceremony, something the Danes had all seen many times before, and whilst a few titters arose at the sight of the king being treated like a baby, it was all done with great dignity, and enough about it was familiar to please them.

'And now that's done,' said Haralt, towelling himself dry, 'I suppose the most important thing is how best to bury the body.'

⊤

Leif was an ash tree. He was an ash tree and something was gnawing at his roots. Claws dug and scratched the length of his trunk; hoofs beat hard upon his branches. How long this went on, he had no idea.

190

The witch-sisters crept slowly down his girth, spiralling the steps of the tree. Two hairy old things with the third dead sister slung between them, swinging by arms and legs, hanging all askew. Two old things creeping in the night, creeping all the way down to Hel. No one else saw them go. And they weren't coming back.

He liked being a tree, he thought. If only all the things on him would try to *hurt* him less. All this passed into darkness.

†

'There's really no point in staying, girl,' Kolga was saying. 'Come on; let's get something to eat.'

'I could sing to him,' Astrid said. 'You've often sung over wounds to heal them.'

'That was then,' said Kolga. 'Before Folkmar broke the stones. After what we've just seen, do you think those old tricks are going to be any good? We'd best trust to Hrafn's herbs and bandages. Come on.'

'I'm not leaving him,' said Astrid. 'I can't just *leave* him.'

The older woman backed away. There was bloody murder in the girl's eyes.

ᚱ

He was a fox cub, trembling in the earth. Something was pacing above the den, and soil scattered on him. It would spoil his perfect fur.

He curled up tighter, wishing that his mother would come

back. But now the something was hopping up and down; the earth was caving in. He mustn't stay there. He had to come out.

He heard the beat of wings as he approached the surface. He thought the angel had come back, and he turned to flee, back down. But his home was gone. There was only soil.

So he looked up, and a black eye returned the look. Stared right into him, direct and painful as an arrow.

It was a raven.

ᚱ

'Astrid,' said Thyre. 'Astrid, come away.'

She laid a hand on her daughter's shoulder – and snatched it away, aghast at the bloody scratches the girl's nails had rent.

'No,' Astrid said.

And through and through her head, a single thought was hammering. Why hadn't she followed him? Why hadn't she been there?

Why hadn't she *done* something?

ᛏ

Leif eyed the raven warily. He didn't like that cruel, curved beak, those heavy talons, and the rising stench of carrion. 'Am I dead, o drinker of the corpse-sea,' he said, 'that you have come to sup upon my flesh?'

The raven opened its beak. '*Greetings, Leif, son of Ibrahim,*' it croaked. '*You have been noticed.*'

192

Leif was confused. The Yelling Stones were gone, broken; he had seen them leave. But no: its eye was alive, not stony. And then he realised who must have sent the huge black bird.

'Greetings to you, and Odin your master.' If he *was* dead, his fate was in Odin's hands. It couldn't hurt to be polite.

The raven ruffled its dark plumage, hopped closer. It was clearly restless. Maybe it was hungry. '*You have won the gods' attention, Half-Dane. Even the High One heard the scream, as it shattered on the angel's sword. A hard fight lies ahead if the North is to be freed of this outlander's pestilence. A pity that your liver proved too weak, when the knife was in your hand.*'

Leif stared back, defiant. 'There's too much blood in this old world of ours.'

'*And more will be shed before this is over.*' The thought seemed to excite the horrid bird, and it jigged about for a moment, snapping its beak.

'So Folkmar lives? He's won?'

'*For now. We will be better prepared for the next battle. In time his whale's carcass, his pig's eyes, will make me quite a meal!*' And it crowed at the prospect.

Leif suddenly felt very, very tired. 'Listen, raven, why are we meeting here? Why in this burrow – why am *I* a fox?'

'*The Yelling Stones sent you visions. They came to pass. This was the vision you sold the Danes. They believed you. So your words created this place. We're in your head, after all.*'

Words, belief, creation . . . if this *was* his head, no wonder it hurt so much. What did the raven want with him? Shouldn't he be in Valhalla by now? Or else, Hel?

And then he understood.

'I'm not dead, am I?' he said.

'*No.*'

'And you're here because . . . because you need me.'

The raven shuffled, from one foot to the other.

'All along, this has been about power. The power of the Yelling Stones, they said. But Folkmar never sought to steal that power. He only wanted people to *believe* – believe in Christ, and not in the old ways. That's where the power comes from, isn't it?'

'*Perhaps.*' The bird's gimlet eye was less ferocious now.

Leif was thinking aloud. 'The power of the stones came –'

'*From the land,*' the raven insisted. '*They wrought their spell from rock and river, tree and earth. They were of the land; from it they drew their power.*'

'Yes, from the land at first – but then it grew, from centuries of worship and belief. That's where the power of the gods lies too; it must be, and that's why you're running scared!' Leif recognised the bird's behaviour now. It wasn't hungry, or excited. It was scared; helpless and scared.

'Both gods and stones have grown strong on belief; on sacrifice and praise and poetry. If that dries up because of Folkmar's words; if all of that belief now goes to Christ . . .'

'*Then we are finished.*' The raven hung its head.

'First the stones asked me for my help. Now you,' he said. 'Because my words help people to believe.'

'*Yes, yes,*' snapped the raven. '*You have the power. But will you use it?*'

194

'I don't think it's my fight any longer,' said Leif. 'I made my choice when I made her the harp.'

'*And then again, when you let fall the knife. But that does not mean it must be over. There are other, lesser knives. And even priests must sleep. You know what you must do.*'

'It seems to me I may do as I please.' Leif's eyes flashed, and his lip curled. 'Now go, before I turn you to an egg!'

The raven edged away a little. '*You would never dare anger the High One so!*'

'Be gone, beggar of death,' Leif began. 'Back to the unborn shell . . .'

With an almighty clatter of wings, the raven bolted.

↓

'Hrafn!' said Kolga. 'I think he's coming round.'

'*What?!*' Astrid sprang to his side.

'Don't crowd him, girl, get back. Give him air . . .'

Leif blinked, moaned, raised his head. His body was one living hurt. Astrid thrust a straw bolster under his head, helping him sit up.

Hrafn was holding a ladle to his lips. 'Drink this,' he said.

'Wassit . . . ?' muttered Leif.

'Broth,' said Hrafn. 'It's good for you.'

Leif struggled to swallow a few mouthfuls of the hot stew. It smelt strongly of leeks, and onions, and made his eyes water.

'Should he really be eating right now?' Astrid hissed to Kolga.

'This is for Hrafn's sake, not his,' Kolga whispered back. 'Once the broth's gone down his body, Hrafn will have a good sniff of his chest. If he can smell the leeks, the burns are deep, and we'll have little chance of saving him.

'But,' she added, forestalling Astrid's explosion, 'if he *can't* smell anything, then there's every chance he'll pull through.'

'Does it hurt terribly?' Astrid asked, turning to Leif.

'Yes, but I'll cope. What's happening over there?'

They all turned back to the burial mound. The crowd had formed two lines, jostling for a better view, leaving a clear path to the hall.

'I've no idea,' said Astrid.

Then Haralt emerged, a group of men behind him. They were carrying spades. 'Dig in from the front, not the top,' the king was saying. 'I want him carried out, not hoisted like a sack of meal.'

THIRTY-TWO

ᚠᚱᛁᛦ᛬ᛏᚢᚠᛁᛦ᛬ᚼᚾ᛬ᛏᚢᛁᛦ

Astrid rose to her feet. 'He's breaking into Father's grave!'

'He's the king now, you can't stop him,' said Kolga, holding her back.

'She's right,' said Leif. 'A king who's seen the light. He'll do what he likes now; he has the power. That miracle will count for quite a lot.'

Astrid was still struggling.

Leif sighed. 'Ah, ah, the pain, the pain!' he screamed. 'It hurts!'

It worked. She turned back, dropped down, mopped his brow.

'Here, in the very place where Bishop Folkmar showed us the path of righteousness, here I will build my church,' Haralt was saying.

He stood between the stones and the mound. 'It will have to be wooden, of course,' he added in an undertone.

'Well, that is fine for the present, naturally, until

stonemasons can be brought from Germany, and you have an excellent supply of forest just the other side of this little hill,' said Folkmar, joining him, and gesturing to the sacred grove – sacred no longer, Astrid realised.

'Let it be so,' agreed Haralt. 'We shall consecrate this ground. And as my first act, not only as a Christian king, but as a dutiful son, I shall extend the blessing of the Lord to my departed father. He shall be buried in the proper fashion, here, beneath the church.'

The crowd fidgeted, unsure. But none would dare challenge Haralt now, in this place, where they had seen the Christ-man's miracle.

'And after the church,' Haralt murmured, as if no one was nearby, 'proper barracks, for an army. An outer wall, like they have in England. That bridge over the marshes and a new route to Ribe. Forts in the north and east . . .'

'We're in, my liege,' said one of the diggers. Men with heavy timbers ran to shore up the opening they had made in the mound.

'Cart the earth out,' the overseer said. 'We'll break through to the chamber soon enough.'

Astrid was fuming.

'Hush, hush, it doesn't matter,' said Leif. 'None of it matters any more.'

'It matters to me,' she said.

'It matters to me too!' Thyre had swept out, and marched towards her son. 'What in Thor's name do you think you're playing at, Haralt?'

'Nothing in Thor's name, Mother,' he replied, his face

serene. 'I'm seeing Father makes it into Heaven.'

'We've hit the chamber!' came a shout, before the queen could say another word.

'At last,' said Haralt. Then, 'Stand back! I will enter first. Weland, walk a step behind me. You will help me carry him out.'

'I have to see, at least,' said Astrid, and slipped from Leif's side.

She was at the front of the crowd behind Haralt, and had a better view than anyone, as the new King of the Danes stepped into his father's grave.

⁝

The wan winter light crept into the burial chamber, thick with dust, and cold, and cobwebs. Astrid hesitated. This was a hundred times worse than being in the hall, or even Thorbjorn's hut.

As Haralt crossed the threshold, Weland a dutiful pace behind his new lord, there was a crunching under his feet. Haralt looked down – a mass of hollow bones, shreds and gobs of gristle clinging to them. All that remained of Hreggskornir, the eagle.

But it would never have rotted away so fast, thought Astrid, *not shut up in here . . .*

Her eyes were adapting to the gloom, and shadows began to peel back from shapes. Slumped over in a corner was the half-devoured carcass of the old grey horse.

Half-devoured?

Then something ran over Astrid's foot, and she jumped.

The unseen thing was crawling up her leg – it was at her ribs – and she might have screamed, but then a tiny voice whispered in her ear.

'Hello, Astrid.'

'Leif?' She squinted, cricking her neck.

A mouse sat on her shoulder. Half the fur was scorched from its body, and both its front paws hung limp, but it seemed happy enough. He must be getting better . . .

She turned back to the tomb.

Haralt was approaching a bed in the centre of the room. A dark figure lay, full-stretched; the body of the king. It seemed massive in that small space. Massive, and black, and still breathing.

Astrid felt the earth closing in on all sides, swallowing her whole.

Haralt bent low over the corpse, and rested a hand on the figure's chest. Instantly, Gorm's eyes snapped open. They glowed: red, fierce and evil.

And now there was total confusion.

'Draugur!' came a cry from behind them, and the Danes at the tunnel's entrance fled. Haralt started back, crossing himself. Astrid leant in for a better sight of her undead father – there was a stumbling push in her back – and the walls of the chamber *did* close, closed like a fist behind her, and they were plunged into utter darkness.

'Trapped,' whispered mouse-Leif.

Then there was silence. Heavy stench. Heavy breathing. She thought someone might be standing just behind her, but didn't dare turn. The only light came from the two red eyes. It burnt brighter, and brighter, and then Gorm rose up from his deathbed.

All the tales she'd ever heard about draugurs, the restless dead, rushed through Astrid's mind. How they had the strength of an ox . . . and the size . . . and the weight. How they snapped the necks of any who disturbed their rest, and ate their flesh. How their appetite was endless.

And now her own father was looming over them, so black he was almost blue, bigger and stronger than she'd ever seen him in life.

For a moment, no one moved.

Then the draugur lunged, too fast to see, huge hands stretching out before him. A snap, a strangled howl; Gorm had seized Weland by the throat and killed him.

The dead king threw back his massive head and laughed. Then he sank his teeth deep into the man's shoulder, and they came away bloody and dripping with flesh. He laughed again, and that was worst of all.

Haralt blundered back, knocking into the chest. He seemed to be groping for something in the darkness – a way out? – as the draugur turned its awful head to Astrid, and she whispered, 'Father?'

There was no recognition in the pitiless red eyes as the thing came on, tossing Weland's body aside.

The mouse dug its tiny hind paws into Astrid's shoulder. 'I'm with you,' it said.

The draugur laughed again, and reached out Hel-black hands.

'No!' shouted Thyre, thrusting Astrid out of the way.

There *had* been someone behind her, and now she stepped between her daughter and her husband, arms flung wide to shield Astrid.

And the air sung, and the steel shone, as Haralt Bluetooth swung the Toledo blade.

THIRTY-THREE

ᚦᚱᛁᛦ·ᛏᛁᚢᛁᛦ·ᚡ·ᚦᚱᛁᛦ

Behind them, winter light flooded back in; the diggers had broken through the chamber wall once more. The head of Gorm the Old rolled on the floor, and the body toppled over, falling heavily on its right side with a crack of bones.

The new king stood, sword in hand. 'Take the head and body out,' he said. 'Folkmar will bury him so that he rises no more – in this kingdom, anyway.'

Thyre glared up at him, holding Astrid, smoothing her hair. 'This is what follows from robbing your father's grave.'

She detached herself from her daughter, and Astrid felt her heart wrench as that soft embrace was broken.

Thyre was spitting with fury. 'This is what comes of desecration, of treachery, of disrespect.'

Haralt made to answer, but she stopped him with a gesture. 'So I'm disowning you, Bluetooth. You don't deserve to bear the name of Gormsson, not after what you've done to my husband. I declare before all this company, here over the body of the last true King of the Danes, that Haralt Bluetooth is no son of mine.'

She bent in closer, defying him to match her stare. 'And you hold your luck too high, Haralt Bluetooth, if you hope to see a hide or hair of *my* half of the kingdom!'

She turned on her heel, and stalked out. 'Jarl Tofi,' she called, 'I would have words with you!'

Haralt's mouth gaped wide as she went. There was a moment's horrified silence.

'He doesn't smell of leeks!' shouted Hrafn.

ᛒ

'But why do you have to *go*?'

'Hush, Astrid, I hate to see you so unhappy –'

'No you don't. You never even look at me!' Astrid said. 'And besides, if you do hate it, then *don't go*!'

Thyre stroked her daughter's sleeve in distraction. 'I can't stay here within smelling distance of that traitor. I should have strangled him at birth . . .'

She breathed hard, blinked, made an effort. 'There's nothing for me here now your father's gone and our faith is lost, Astrid; I would have left anyway.'

'But where will you go? Back out east?'

'No. Just to Baekke.'

'With Jarl Tofi?' Astrid's eyes widened.

'Of course. I might even marry him. We'll see.'

Well, thought Astrid. *That* explained a lot.

'I've not yet seen forty summers,' went on Thyre. 'I've still got a life to lead, you know. I'm not just going to . . . fade away.'

'But what about me?' It sounded more like a whine than she'd meant it to.

'You could come with me.'

'No,' said Astrid. 'I can't leave Leif.'

'Then, when his wounds have healed . . . ?'

'You'd have us both?'

Thyre paused. 'Listen, child. I know your brothers – I mean, Knut and . . . and Haralt – were wanting to marry you off. To the wrong men, to be sure. But, Astrid, one day soon, you *must* marry –'

'Mother –'

'And not to please any man. But for your own good. Look at me. I was nothing; a good girl from a fine family yes, but *nothing* in myself, before I married your father. And now – lands, wealth, power – they're all *mine*. By right. And no man can take them from me. Do you see?'

'But I don't *want* –'

'Astrid, the law is clear. Until you marry, you're no better than . . . than a horse, or a house, and a lot less useful. But once you do, you can *own* horses, and houses. Suddenly, you matter. I want you to matter.'

'And will the law stay the same, once Haralt makes us all Christians?'

'I don't know. Astrid, dear heart, all I'm saying is, that boy is brave, and bright, and a better man than most. But he's got nothing to offer you.'

205

'By Heimdall's horn, Mother, I'm not about to *marry* him! I like him, that's all.'

'Is it?'

'And right now,' said Astrid, ignoring the question, 'he needs me. Which is more than you do.'

ᚠ

The queen rode out in spite of the snow, a stream of Tofi's followers before and behind, beating clear the path from Jelling. She never once looked back.

'This could mean trouble, in the days to come,' muttered Arinbjorn, the old Norwegian.

Haralt merely stared after her.

'If it is pleasing to Your Majesty,' said Folkmar, 'I have been thinking. You have a claim in law, as the rightful heir of Gorm, to the *whole* realm – her half and his half.'

'Yes . . . ?' said Haralt.

'And this is relying, is it not, on that which we all know: Thyre is your mother and was Gorm's wife.'

'A claim she will now dispute, having disowned me.'

'Then why not say the truth? Why not say so in writing, for all to see?'

'I hardly think,' said Haralt, 'that in days to come, the Danes will line up to peer into some book, to learn the truth of the matter.'

'Your Majesty, I was not thinking of any book,' said Folkmar. He pointed at the two remaining Yelling Stones.

The stones stood, forlorn, but still solid great shapes,

between the king's hall and the spot where Gorm was being reburied, where Haralt's first church would be built. At the very centre of his kingdom.

Folkmar smiled. 'You Northmen write upon rocks, do you not?'

↑

The winter was turning. Haralt announced that as soon as the ice broke on Lake Faarup, he would march the whole court down and baptise them on its banks.

Leif was healing fast enough to be among those marchers. Though both his hands still hung limp, his body was nearly whole again.

It's me who has the power, he told himself. *It comes from within me.* And he looked at his livid red chest, and spoke secret words to the skin, and all the time, he healed.

'Is it over?' asked Astrid. 'Have we lost?' She was keen to be off, now there was nothing left to fight for. She was sure that the mass baptism would mean her own betrothal.

'I'm not quite sure,' said Leif. 'It feels like it.'

He was wholly wrapped up in his new knowledge. He was not a tool of remote gods or ancient stones, but a part of things. Part of the land. Powerful in his own right. If he knew a thing, it was his friend. This was all too exciting for him to care much about the king and his bishop right now. But he had no idea how to express this to Astrid without sounding like a complete fool.

'Shall we walk?' she said. For he was walking now, with her help.

They paced the still-white courtyard. Men were clustered around the two stones. They heard the sound of a hammer and chisel.

'Closer,' said Leif, and they hobbled to where they had a better view.

'It's done,' said a man, and moved back from the smaller stone. Leif and Astrid read the runes, carved deep into the rock.

'King Gorm made this monument for Thyre, his wife . . . *what*?' said Astrid, and rushed round the other side.

She ran back to Leif. '. . . his wife, adornment of the Dane-mark,' she finished, furious.

'But it's a lie! A lie to prove that Haralt is her heir!'

'Shh,' said Leif, as heads turned. 'I don't think it can help to say so now.'

'But how can they even *do* that?' she hissed. 'I thought they were powerful witches, these stones, everyone was scared of them!'

'They're just stones now,' he said, and walked forward. No more talk of gods, he thought. He was flesh and bone; he was one with the earth. 'Land's teeth; heath-ribs; two silent sentinels.' He reached out to touch the larger stone, with the naked palm of his half-bandaged left hand.

A second carver was etching on it the image of a man, hanging from what looked like branches, feet together, arms outspread. It was beautiful. He could admit that now. It was over. He touched the stone.

And reeled back with a cry of pain.

Astrid rushed to catch him as he fell. 'What is it?'

Leif clapped his swaddled hands to his ears. 'Stop stop stop,' he said.

'Stop *what*?'

'I can feel it. Every single stroke. It cuts, Astrid, it cuts so very deep!'

The chisel bit, again and again, and Leif twisted as if his own ribs were splintering under the impact.

He *knew* the stone, and this was what that meant. Every blow of the hammer, to etch that beautiful man – he shared it with the stone.

And in his head was the chisel's song – the song of the tool as it worked. Folkmar's song. Haralt's song.

'Quarry the rock,
Fell the oak,
Gouge the land,
Build build build.
Quarry the rock,
Fell the oak,
Gouge the land,
Build build build!'

Breathing hard as a spent horse, he shut out the gleeful tune. Mastered the shard-shattering pain. And he turned to Astrid, and he said, 'No.'

'No?'

'It's not over. We may have lost. But it's not over.'

And he remembered something then.

He still had one of his three choices left to make.

Astrid couldn't understand it. 'It's just a church, Leif. You had one at Hedeby – why are you so interested in how it's built?'

'I'm learning.'

'You're annoying, that's what you are. Why are we still here? You can walk again, you can ride . . . well, you can sit on a horse. We should leave. We're free now, Leif.' And her face shone like a second sun at the thought.

'Tell that to Haralt. He has plans for you.'

'That's why we should just go now. In the night. Not even Haralt would think of anyone else leaving before spring comes.'

'I can't call myself free until it's done.'

He was obsessed with this church. Every day he walked around the building site, trailing his broken hands against objects. Fingering the fittings. Talking to the craftsmen, and the women working on what would go inside. Laying his cheek against the beams.

They had cut down half the grove to provide the timber. Mostly ancient oaks for the frame, and younger hazels for the wall panels. Astrid was not the only one to shed hot tears as the axes sung, and the trees toppled, but Leif remained calm, following each tree from its felling, to its resting place in the body of the church.

Just what the Hel was he up to, thought Astrid.

At last it was done.

'I am thinking I shall live in the church,' said Folkmar, 'until I have a proper congregation. It would be a crime, to give this house of God to the little mice alone.'

'It would be as great a crime for you to *live* alone, bishop,' said Haralt, his face wreathed in smiles. That in itself was a sign of danger.

His words now rose to take in the whole hall. 'And so it is my wish,' Haralt went on, 'that, to comfort you in your work, and as a sign of the love between my family and that of your kinsman, King Otto, that I give you –'

'*Skita*,' whispered Astrid. It had come at last.

'That I give you the hand in marriage of the only kin I have left to me. My sister, Astrid.' She just had time to turn to Leif, before they led her to the high table. 'Stuff your plan. We leave at first light.'

ᚼ

'It's all prepared. We're packed. Hestur's ready.'

'And Valvigs is with him,' said Astrid. 'I've got my harp. Now all we need is a decent sleep. I'm pretty sure I can wake before the dawn.'

'Just check the bags,' he said. 'You're good with knots.'

She turned, bending over the twin sacks of dried food, silver trinkets and warm clothing.

As Leif looked down at her, he thought of something they'd once said to each other.

'*Please . . . Astrid . . . trust me?*'

211

'*All right,*' *said Astrid.* '*All right. I trust you.*'

And he blinked away a tear, as he gripped a log from near the fire between his palms, and brought it down on the back of her head.

'There's just one thing I have to do,' he whispered to her fallen form.

It was hard. But he thought of the stones' pain at the blows of the chisel, of the butchered troll, and of all the deaths that might still come if Folkmar wasn't put in his place.

And he set down the log, and strode, silent, from the room.

THIRTY-FOUR

ᚦᚱᛁᛦ·ᛏᛁᚵᛁᛦ·ᚡᛁᛦ·ᚡᛁᛅᛦᛁᛦ

Large and low, the church loomed up before him. Leif smiled. First had come the Yelling Stones, back in the bad old days. Then the giants' stone-ship, the mound, the hall – and now this. All because people had always been drawn to this spot. But these monuments weren't witnesses to the power of gods, or witches, but to the strength of those who had built them. This church might have been raised in honour of Folkmar's Christ. But it had been made by human hands, and he had been there, and seen it done.

He was not afraid.

But his heart jolted as two ghostly shapes flitted out of the church. He ducked into shadows, grateful for his dark skin. The shapes were two girls – thralls – Fala and Feima.

He held his breath as they went by. Good. They couldn't have seen him.

Leif pushed them from his mind; they'd left the church door ajar, and he snuck inside.

213

His eyes widened, searching to see in the ill-lit room.

There wasn't much to the building, just a nave and a chancel, an inner square of pillars stretching up into the blackness. Oil lamps flickered, uncertain and dim, and the air hung heavy with sharp foreign scents, overlying a nastier, less exotic smell.

The chancel, where the altar was, was shut off by a screen, hanging from a cross-beam, on which was carved a cross. The screen itself was only linen; Haralt's first church was a rough and ready affair. Folkmar was using that part to sleep in, until the Danes were baptised and he had a congregation.

Something was stirring behind the screen.

Leif tiptoed over, his skin crawling as he crossed the fresh-dug grave of twice-dead Gorm. Cautiously, he lifted a corner of the screen, and peered through.

Folkmar was kneeling with his face to the altar, dressed in a hairy brown shirt – a far cry from the robes he wore around the court. He was holding a many-thonged crop.

And it was this crop he raised, as he turned to look Leif full in the eye.

'Ah, the little poet. I presume this is not a social call . . . ?'

'We have a score to settle, you and I,' said Leif.

Folkmar groped behind him, till his searching fingers found his massive crook. Leaning heavily against it, he rose to his full height. In that small space, he towered over the boy.

'You cannot think I am afraid! You hardly have the use of your hands.' He brandished the crook in the boy's face.

Leif glanced at the massive staff. *If I know a thing, then it is my friend.* 'Gold is snuggest in rock – go back to the river.

Shimmer for your own sake; scorn this greedy master,' he said.

Folkmar gaped, as the heavy gilt head of his crook softened, streamed to the floor, and was gone. Then he recovered, reversing his weapon, levelling its wicked iron point at the boy.

'We're both born of this land,' said Leif, to the iron. 'Be not hard for the soft.'

The iron, too, vanished, and Folkmar was left holding a plain wooden staff. Grimly, the priest shifted his grip, and swung it at Leif's head. But Leif had done this one before.

'Ash, be yourself again.'

As the staff swung, it budded and blossomed, twigs and leaves shooting forth. Folkmar lost his hold, and it flew away, striking the wall, a small tree now clinging to the timbers of the church.

The priest flicked his eyes back to the boy – but Leif had let fall the screen, and was gone. Folkmar tugged it aside and stepped across, into the nave, staring hard.

Leif darted behind one of the wooden pillars. He whispered to the oil lamps, 'Why flit so fast, young bloods? For night gives rest to all.' And, as one, they went out.

It was almost too easy.

Now the only light in the church came from the lamps behind the altar; in front of Folkmar, darkness pooled.

'You are rash to quarrel, boy – have I not displayed the strength of my God?'

'You seemed to favour the strength of your staff,' said Leif, flitting from one pillar to another. 'What are you going to do now – squash me?'

For the first time, Folkmar smiled. 'Phanuel?' he called.

And up among the rafters, something stirred. Leif glanced up, seeing nothing. But he could hear a scratch, and a rustle, as of the unfurling of enormous wings.

ᚠ

Leif froze. His whole plan hinged on what he had learnt: that power came from belief. He had to *not* believe in the angel if he was to defeat Folkmar. But then, wasn't fear a form of belief?

The heavy, spiced air stirred as the wings started to beat, and up above, a light began to glow.

'Where are the flippant remarks now?' called Folkmar, and Leif bit his lip.

'Where are your Odin and your Thor? Let them show themselves, and Christ will strike them down, as Archangel Phanuel has struck down the demons of this pagan land!'

The light was swelling. The angel was near. It was coming for him. Leif closed his eyes, felt the cool wood against his back.

From belief, came power. The pagan Danes had been quick to accept Folkmar, with his Christ and his angel. Leif had to reject that.

But it wasn't just belief: it was fear. That was how belief got in. As a small child, Leif had once been afraid of the dark. He had beaten that fear.

Now, he needed to defeat his fear of the light.

'Descend!' cried Folkmar, and the angel landed. Whiteness filled the room. Leif heard the thud of heavy feet on clay,

216

and the crackle and rasp as the burning sword was drawn. In his mind's eye he saw the perfect, beautiful, hideous face turn in his direction, staring cold and pure through the pillar. In two heartbeats, it would come for him.

Beat one.

And Leif stepped from his hiding place, straight into the circle of light.

†

That terrible head swivelled towards him, a spear's length away, perfect mouth opening to scream.

'You know, I think I've had enough of gods,' said Leif. And he turned his back on it, to address Folkmar. 'Of angels, draugurs, visions, all of that.'

He could feel the beast's breath on his neck, hot and dry, the arid wind of deserts and of dust. He tried to ignore it. *I've no faith in your god; you can't hurt me.* But if he turned, or if he ran, he was done for.

'I've had enough of all the silly games that men like you and Knut and Haralt play. The prayers, the fights, the power that you crave.' Folkmar's face was one fat puzzle.

'I had a sword, and I gave it away,' said Leif. 'I couldn't care less about "souls" and "sin". The best thing that I did was for a girl.'

And he took a step towards the priest.

'If power lies for you in secret books, and in the burning blade of your winged pet, then so be it. Just don't think I'm impressed.'

Another step. He no longer felt the breath on his back.

'I'm no hero. I wasn't raised by dwarfs. My skin is dark. I call no king my kin.'

With each sentence, another step.

'*My* power lies in words that all men know, in calling kin the trees, the earth, the stones. In understanding what it is I touch; the nature of the things I need to live.'

Behind him, the harsh white light was dimming.

'You think this is your church. But where were you when it was being built? Tucked up inside, too busy saying prayers, and praising kings, and stuffing your fat face to even watch!'

Leif smiled then. 'But *I* watched, and my hands ran through the flax they spun into that screen. I saw each tree as it was being felled, and smelt its bark, and held it while the tools were hard at work. I trod the clay beneath my bare feet, as it was being laid wet from the river.'

As Leif said 'flax', the linen screen stirred, and wound itself around Folkmar's quivering body.

As he said 'tree', the planks from either wall stretched out new branches, and seized Folkmar's hands.

And as he said 'clay', the floor itself grew hands, and took firm hold of each of Folkmar's ankles.

The priest was stammering, spitting, struggling to speak. His eyes avoided Leif's, straining to see into the returning darkness. 'O, Phanuel . . .' he gasped.

'"O, Phanuel"! *Is that even his name?*'

Fear, defiance, even hope, all danced across Folkmar's features. 'Then get on with it, damn you. But know this: my work will not end with me. Kill me, and my soul is going

218

to Heaven. But on earth, more will come to tame this land. Priests! Angels! And a thousand thousand German spears! So do not think I am afraid of death.'

'Oh no. I think you'd like that far too much. To be a "martyr", then to be a "saint". Oh yes, you see I know the words. Back home, a better Christian than you'll ever be described to me the good parts of your creed. That's why I know just what to do with you.'

'Listen, boy –'

'*My name is Leif*. The son of Ibrahim. And I –' and here Leif leant in very close, so near that he could smell the red wine and veal on Folkmar's breath – '*and I forgive you*.'

Folkmar reeled, coughed, retching for air. As Leif turned on his heel the linen, wood and clay let go their hold on their prisoner.

'I forgive you, Folkmar,' he called back over his shoulder. 'Remember that, when you baptise the Danes. I had you in my power, *twice,* and I showed *mercy*.'

As Leif strode from the church, Folkmar wheezed, red-faced, clutching at his chest. If the angel still stood in the shadows, or if not, Leif never even noticed.

THIRTY-FIVE

ᚦᚱᛁᚱ᛬ᛏᛁᚢᛁᚱᚼᛁ᛬ᚠᛁᛏ

Leif awoke at first light to find a spear at his throat. Well, that settled it: the witch had been right. His third choice had been wrong as well . . .

From somewhere nearby, Astrid was groaning as she came to, her head throbbing. Leif sighed. 'He didn't choose to turn the other cheek,' he muttered, as two mail-clad men hauled him to his feet.

He was dragged before a bleary-eyed Haralt. Few other people were about so early; the dawn was grey, cheerless, muted.

'Where's Folkmar?' said Leif.

'Bishop Folkmar,' replied Haralt, 'is dead.'

ᚱ

Leif's eyes widened. 'Dead?'

'Silence! A thrall found his body when he carried in his

breakfast. The bishop likes – *liked* – to be woken early, with a cooked meal.'

'I'll bet he did,' came a low snigger nearby, and Haralt glared.

'He was found slumped upon the altar – *upon the altar!* – with his hands clutching at his chest and throat, and an expression of supreme pain upon his face. The body was quite cold. And *you* –' Here the king stood, and pointed a damning finger, apoplectic with rage. '*You* were seen in the dead of night, breaking into the church, and by God you will pay with your life!'

For the first time, Leif noticed the two thralls, Feima and Fala, cowering, avoiding his eye. And then Astrid exploded.

'*I* killed him, King Haralt,' she shouted, stepping between Leif and her brother.

Even in the heat of the moment, she had wits enough to stamp down on Leif's foot, turning his protest into a yowl of pain. She'd have to be quick, if this was to work.

'I killed him, not Leif, and I'll swear it on . . . on the Cross, or his old book, or a silver ring or clod of earth or whatever poxy thing you want me to, I'll swear it. And you'll take my word above that of a pair of thralls. You have to. That's the law.'

'But how . . . ?' said Haralt, sinking back into his throne.

'I . . .' She snatched at a stray memory. 'I took henbane from the garden, back at midsummer! I've been saving it up, in case you ever asked me to marry Folkmar. I put it in his wine!'

She was on the edge of tears. Behind her, Leif tried to

speak again. Without looking, she drove an elbow back into his ribs.

Her head felt like Thor had hit it with his hammer. And that was Leif's fault. He'd betrayed her trust for the sake of revenge – but what did that matter, against everything else he'd done? She could forgive him that.

They could hang her if they liked. But at least, this time, she had been there for him. She would not let him down.

Haralt mopped his brow. 'Astrid, Astrid. You are all the kin I have left . . .'

He stood once more. 'I cannot send my own flesh and blood to the gallows. I, who have lost father, mother and brother in so cruel and swift a fashion, cannot condemn to death all that remains of my family.'

The tension sagged loose in the hall.

'But,' Haralt went on, 'I cannot let so foul a crime go unpunished. Astrid Gormsdottir, you are found guilty of murder by your own admission. As punishment, you are banished from my kingdom.

'You have one month to leave the land of the Danes. After that time, if ever you set foot inside my realm, your life will be forfeit, and any man may kill or enslave you without fear of censure from the law. Now get out of my sight.'

She bowed her head, heart still racing.

'Oh, and, Leif,' Haralt added, as he turned to leave the hall.

'Yes, my liege?'

'You're banished too.'

THIRTY-SIX

ᚦᚱᛁᚱ·ᛏᛁᚠᛁᚱ·ᛅ·ᚴᚴ

It was the first day of spring. Dawn rose low behind the dunes, and somewhere, a curlew called a welcome. The strip of white sand ran away on either hand, fading out of sight to north and south, and to the west rolled the green-grey ocean.

Two figures trod the lonely shore. One led a horse; the other held a falcon. Together they stopped. Together, they watched the pale sunlight strike the breaking waves.

'This must be the great sea-longing,' one said.

'We're free at last,' said the other. 'We can go *anywhere*. How about Iceland? You always used to go on about Iceland . . .'

'"To Iceland or anywhere . . ."'

'To Iceland or anywhere!' And they laughed.

The falcon mewled, impatient.

'Let's let him out. He might even catch us breakfast . . .'

Astrid let slip the hood, and the white bird soared, higher

and higher and ever higher, till white was black against the scudding clouds. Its cry was harsh, and young, and free. They watched as it wrote circles on the sky.

HISTORICAL NOTE

THE YELLING STONES is a true story. Well, more or less. The two stones still stand, between the church and the mound, in Jelling. Though now, unlike when first I saw them, they're trapped within glass.

I have taken events of 958–63 and squeezed them into a single year. Gorm, Thyre, Haralt and Knut all lived and – in two cases – died much as they do in the book. Knut was shot in an ambush when preparing to attack Dublin. Haralt succeeded his father as king, moving Gorm's body from the mound to the church, burying him with his favourite cup. Gorm's bones bear what might be the marks of his final encounter with his son. Scholars still argue over whether Gorm wrote the runes on the smaller stone for Thyre, or if Haralt had them forged.

Folkmar really was the missionary who braved an ordeal to convert the Danes. Better known by his nickname, 'Poppo', he lived to reap an earthly reward, becoming archbishop of Cologne. All the beliefs, practices, events, places, and most of the people – Jarl Tofi, Egil Skallagrimsson, Arinbjorn, Haakon of Norway, Grey-cloak, King Otto, even Leif's father – are real too. Only Leif and Astrid have escaped the attention of historians. Until now.

One last thing. The runes scattered throughout this book contain a hidden message. It is the message written on the smaller of the stones of Jelling – which Astrid reads on page 208.

ACKNOWLEDGEMENTS

Thank you to everyone involved in the making of this book. To everyone at Hot Key, especially Jenny and above all my marvellous editor, Emma. To Joanna, who first hoiked me from the slush pile – I have put you in the books! To Jules, to Stephanie and my agent Chris, without whose indefatigable resolve, nous and good cheer, none of this would be.

To Lesley Abrams, a legend-worthy tutor who rekindled my Nordic passion. To Kate, who gave frank advice, and David, who honed the final sentence.

To my Mama and Papa, my Oma and my sister Freyja, on whose love and assistance most of my life, including this book, may be blamed. To Emma, who read over every word before even I did, and was sure to praise first, and criticise later. And to Nils Jensen, my Opa, who told me the stories.

OSKAR JENSEN

Oskar was born, and lives, which is always nice. Having spent the seven years since school studying history in Oxford, he has finally escaped to London, where he and his girlfriend live the dream, or at least a dream, in a little Bloomsbury flat. When not writing novels about Norsemen (and women), playing five-a-side football or various instruments, Oskar moonlights (full-time) as a post-doctoral researcher in the Music Department of King's College London. It's all very confusing. Having squandered years of writing on student journalism, and, even worse, student poetry, most of his literary efforts are now either academic, or songs, or both. Find out more at oskarjensen.com

HOT KEY BOOKS

Thank you for choosing a Hot Key book.

If you want to know more about our authors and what we publish, you can find us online.

You can start at our website

www.hotkeybooks.com

And you can also find us on:

We hope to see you soon!